FIRST-NAME BASIS

DJ HICKS

First Edition

ISBN: 978-1-960146-45-8 (hard cover)
      978-1-960146-46-5 (soft cover)

Editor: Karli Jackson

Published by Warren Publishing
Charlotte, NC
www.warrenpublishing.net
Printed in the United States

To my past, current, and future family,
thank you for putting up with me
and leaving me alone to read.
And now write.

All love.

"pray for _____"

PROLOGUE

What's the use?

Did you say your prayers today? Maleek, are you doing what's right? Are you living in the light of God? What if his light has never reached me? I feel fine living in the shadows. They have treated me well, and they are more consistent than anything I hear people yell at me on the street. Those stories they told us in Sunday school don't age very well. Removing the war, plague, and death from those stories doesn't prepare you for the real world. It's all distorted. Where is the truth in those words? I'm sure he exists somewhere between those words and our interpretation of them, but I haven't seen him in some time, if ever. How can I place my trust in someone I've never seen? That's why I trust in me. If I succeed, it's on my shoulders. If I fail, it's because my feet stumbled. I would never blame my failures on someone else—they see him as the ultimate scapegoat.

Maybe that's the reason: the more people pray the less accountability they feel for their place in life. It's that, *Oh, I prayed about it,* reasoning that I can't get with. How can you pray for God's help and then you won't even help yourself? I hate to see people live their life through a prayer. Your life is to be lived. Not just prayed for. And what about those skipped days? Those days where life comes at you from all sides and there is no prayer to protect you. Is God still there for you? Or did he take that day off too? That's why I keep my foot to the pedal and control my own days. They want all their days to be filled with sunshine but they're afraid to walk outside and get burnt. My skin is burnt. On the inside and outside. I've got a condo in the valley and a view on the mountaintop. Wherever I go, I'm ready for what's waiting for me, not because I prayed about it, but because I've lived it. Came out on the other side better for it. I know she thinks that those times hardened my heart, changed me for the worse. But what's wrong with a little extra protection? She views it as a deformity. I see it as growth. Bones grow back stronger after they are broken. So why pray for no broken bones?

Why not pray for the opportunity to break bones? To break free? To move away from comfort and into challenges. That's not what I hear. That's not what I feel. No need to make a scene though. No need to "embarrass" her as she shouts through her silence. I know she loves me more than I can understand, and I love her more than I know how to show. Her love is tangible. That's one thing I can feel: her urge for me to become who she thinks I need to be. It comes from an internal well of love but reaches the surface like a mama bird shoving her baby out of the nest. Good intentions. Harsh results. Good thing I was ready to fly.

I can feel the benefit of her love now. But *his* love, this unconditional love I hear of, I'm still waiting for my return on investment. I admit, I haven't invested much in that relationship for the past handful of years, but what about those early years? My interest should be accruing still. I should see those residuals. Or does the well dry up fast? If he stops hearing from me, does he start to skim from the top? Do my blessings slowly wash away from the shore if I'm not there actively trying to catch them all before the currents take them to someone else's section of the beach? That seems exhausting. And that's the issue. We pray and we pray and we pray. We stress and we stress and we stress. We wait and we wait and we wait. And his answers could be out there. Floating in the tide. Coming close to tempt us with an appearance of breakthrough, only then to be pulled away harshly in mockery. It peeks its head above the waves to tease us with everything we could become. Everything we could have. Then dips back under to keep us questioning if we ever truly saw it. Did we see it? It's right over this next wave. It's coming in the one after that. So we wait on the shore. Anticipating our answered prayers to roll up like a message in a bottle with news of health and wealth on the way. Did this message come from him? Or from someone else farther up the shore?

I don't plan to wait and see. I'd rather take a dip.

–Maleek Wright

CHAPTER ONE
The Stage

Periwinkle. Hmm. Lavender? Wine. No. It's not so strong. It's somewhere in there. I could ask every person who goes to this church and get a different answer. That's the fun and the bad of the stage. Everyone has their own opinion. I hear Marcus does a well-enough job. As long as the money keeps coming in, I suppose is how it goes. They've been "New Haven" for what, six or seven years now? I didn't know churches went through rebrands. Makes sense. People want something new and exciting. Something different than the meal they had yesterday. The flock is hard to keep happy.

Yet, all that change, and they kept this jam-colored stage. Maybe it has some special meaning. Maybe it was too expensive to replace. It hides enough of the dirt—which I hate. How am I supposed to tell when it's clean? I liked marked improvement. Sure, I can get the noticeable dust bunnies and pieces of dirt tracked in from the various shoes that grace this stage, but you can't see those things twenty rows back anyhow. But I get it, if this was the centerpiece of my house, I'd go out of my way to show special attention to it as well. One week I'm going to "miss a few spots" and see if there is any commotion from the staff. I've barely received a single comment in my three years cleaning this place. Not one additional request. Not one *can we do better here?* I don't even know if they check the work! They're probably afraid of coming off as condescending. Christians seem to struggle with that: confrontation. Or being too confrontational. Or maybe I'm just that good.

The people here do seem to get along well, for a church at least. I hear about the big moments and stories connecting these strangers. I recognize a few of them out in the town. It's usually a polite wave or one of those big smiles that does all the talking for you. I appreciate it. We don't know each other really. I'm the janitor they happen to run into around their church building, not their coach or classmate or friend or family member. They have their lives to live and their prayers to make and valleys to go through and mountaintops to shine on. Or something like that. I should probably listen to a few more services at some point. Just in case one of them did ever stop me in public and ask if I go here like that little girl almost did at the grocery store last year. Kids have no shame like that. I come here, yes. I come to this magenta stage and ensure it's the smoothest piece of carpet you ever saw in your life. I come and search through the crooks and crannies and cracks in the parking lot and drips in the kitchen and eliminate the mess in front of me. Cleanliness is next to godliness. I know that much.

No. Plum.

DAY: SUNDAY, JANUARY 3
TIME: 12:17 P.M.
LOCATION: NEW HAVEN STAGE

Lord, we come to you humbly and grateful for another year on this beautiful planet. And we thank you for the opportunity to continue to grow and commit ourselves to building your kingdom in this new year. I pray our church is faithful in the mission you have called us to. I pray we never lose sight of that mission and that through all the highs and lows this year is sure to bring, we remain faithful to you. Help us bring the graduations, the sickness, the love, the pain, the breakups and the breakdowns—help us bring all of it to your feet, Lord. Because that's where you pick us up and make us whole. It's where we are reminded of our constant need for you in our lives. Not just as our therapist, but as our father, as our shepherd, our provider, and as our redeemer. Lord, please help us remain close to you throughout this year and help us lead those afar back into your house. Let us be bold in our faith and proclaim it proudly. Give us the strength to be the light in the lives of those around us day in and day out. We thank you for putting our church right here in this community right now. Thank you for your presence in this building. Thank you for your unconditional love. And all of God's people said ... amen.

Source: Marcus Garland, 43

Day: Monday, January 4
Time: 8:47 a.m.
Location: Salister Driveway

God, please let there be no traffic on the way to work today. I could really do without my boss on my ass.

Appreciate it.

Source: Augustus Salister, 32

Day: Tuesday, January 5
Time: 12:05 p.m.
Location: Oak Creative Design Agency Bathroom Stall

I don't know anymore, God, I thought I was done with this last year. Please help me see me how you see me ... please help me come to terms with how I look, and be comfortable in my skin. I don't want to be fake anymore. I don't want to be fat anymore, just take this weight away from me ... please ... I don't want to spend my lunches in stalls anymore. I want to be healthy. I want to be me.

Source: Bri Verdana, 29

Day: Wednesday, January 6
Time: 6:47 p.m.
Location: Faulkner Dining Table

Uhh, Jesus ... please bless this food. And bless Mommy. And bless Daddy. And my big brother Salem. And bless my basketball team. We need to win soon, Jesus. Thank you for this chicken. Thank you for these potatoes. And I guess thank you for broccoli, too, even though I don't like it much. And, yeah, amen.

Source: Izzy Faulkner, 6

Day: Friday, January 8
Time: 6:45 a.m.
Location: Many Men Bible Study (Chaucer Kitchen)

God, we welcome you into this place right now and pray that this time we're able to spend together brings us closer to you and helps us become better disciples of your word. We thank you for the health of everyone in this room and we ask that you look over our families and spouses. Thank you again for this opportunity to meet in your name freely and for the doughnuts Malcolm brought today.

Source: Keith Chaucer, 34

DAY: SATURDAY, JANUARY 9
TIME: 7:51 P.M.
LOCATION: LANSING LIVING ROOM

God, please look after Maleek tonight as he goes out to work. You know I worry about his physical and mental health. Please help him open up and let him know he can talk to me about anything. Place your guidance and protection over him.

Source: Gigi Lansing, 82

DAY: SUNDAY, JANUARY 10
TIME: 8:13 A.M.
LOCATION: NEW HAVEN PARKING LOT

God, thank you for another opportunity to deliver your message to this congregation. Please speak through me today and open the ears and hearts of our church. Please give me the courage and strength to stand up for you today and every day. Help me to not focus on my faults and weaknesses but on the greatness and awesome ability you bring to every situation. Thank you for everything.

Thank you for a partner who supports me no matter how well I preach. She's my rock. Thanks for a son who, well, who acts like he cares at least—ha. I pray this is a better year for us than last year. We need something to share that isn't in this building. I don't want his only memories of us to be me on the stage. He's too important to me for the shallow relationship we have right now.

Amen.

Source: Marcus Garland, 43

DAY: MONDAY, JANUARY 11
TIME: 3:48 A.M.
LOCATION: CLAREMORE BUS-STATION BENCH

God ... I don't know if you're still there. I don't know how you could do this to me. I never hurt anybody. I don't understand what I did to deserve this—just do something, God. Do what you do for everyone else.

Source: Ulises Zind, 41

DAY: TUESDAY, JANUARY 12
TIME: 8:32 A.M.
LOCATION: SCHOOL BUS #44

Jesus, thank you for today. Thank you for my friends. I don't want to ask this, but please help my dad decide to do something else. I don't want him to do what he does anymore. People look at me weird. My friends don't want to come over. Please help him be a firefighter or something everyone likes.

Source: Jonah Garland, 15

DAY: WEDNESDAY, JANUARY 13
TIME: 8:13 P.M.
LOCATION: FORT MIND HIGH SCHOOL GIRLS LOCKER ROOM

Lord, we thank you for this day. We thank you for this opportunity to play this great game in your name. We pray that you keep us healthy and upright out on the court tonight. Let us play for each other. Let us compete to the best of our abilities. Give us the strength and stamina to play a complete game. We pray for all the loose balls and all the lucky bounces. And let us walk away with this righteous victory—

BIG WUBS!

Yes, Lord, let us walk away with big wubs tonight.

AYYYYE!

In your name we play, amen.

Source: Layla Sacron, 17

Day: Thursday, January 14
Time: 8:37 p.m.
Location: Faulkner Bedroom

Please protect my family this year. I don't know why I have a feeling that a storm is coming, but maybe that's just me being an anxious parent. I remember I told myself I would never be the dad who overworried about every little thing, and yesterday I followed Izzy's bus to the school. I never thought I'd be that dad! I'm still not a fan of the bus scene, I'd rather just take her myself, but my wife says it's good for her "socializing"—like she isn't everyone's best friend after five seconds. Everyone adores her. We will need to fix that when the boys start coming around. Please make her a book nerd or something, God. I can't even think about that time ... yikes.

Source: Michael Faulkner, 37

Day: Friday, January 15
Time: 11:48 a.m.
Location: Vintage Spirits Third-Floor Cubicle

It's your partially faithful servant, Jesus. Don't you love my sense of humor? Well, you know what I would love? For this presentation to go well. Not for me, I'm not *that* selfish. But so I can get a raise, to then use that money on my terror—I mean joy—of a new stepson. I could really use some goodwill with him these days. I think I saw him plotting my disappearance on his phone last week. I know I will never be his dad, but I can at least try to do dad things for him. Like ... oh no, I don't even know what dads do. Damn. Sorry. I'm really trying not to mess this up with his mom, though, and, well ... him. Please help me nail this presentation so I can afford to take him to a game or something. Do kids still like sports? Oh, God, I hope so.

Source: Kenny Sturgiss, 37

DAY: SATURDAY, JANUARY 16
TIME: 10:17 A.M.
LOCATION: HANOI PLAYROOM

Mr. Christ, please put my favorite show on this morning. I need it today.

Source: Victor Hanoi, 7

TIME: 10:32 A.M.
LOCATION: HANOI PLAYROOM

What the heck, Mr. Christ.

Source: Victor Hanoi, 7

Day: Sunday, January 17
Time: 9:09 P.M.
Location: Curtis Bedroom

Lord, we come to you again this year completely believing in your ability to perform miracles, in your ability to do great things for those who believe in you, completely believing in your desire to grow your kingdom ... and grow this belly. We pray that you help us remain patient for the gift of a child, and that you help us prepare to be the best parents possible for our little nugget—
Jacobe.
And please help us have a girl so we don't have to name her *Jacobe* ....
Hey, you said—
Amen.
Amen ... I guess ....

Source: Tricia Curtis, 31, and Graham Curtis, 29

Day: Monday, January 18
Time: 11:44 A.M.
Location: Mrs. Laslo's Class (Rose Mound Middle School Classroom 11A)

Dear God, help my stepdad just ... chill out a bit. I know he's trying to be supportive, but he's trying too hard. I don't need texts in every class wishing me good luck. Especially with Mrs. Laslo. Help her chill out too.

Source: Hauz Metzen, 14

Day: Tuesday, January 19
Time: 11:45 a.m.
Location: Mrs. Laslo's Class (Rose Mound Middle School
Classroom 11A)

I swear, God, if one more kid farts in my direction I'm going to get kicked out of this hellhole.

Source: Bailey Laslo, 39

Day: Thursday, January 21
Time: 1:30 a.m.
Location: Quino Backyard

Watch over my nephew, Jesus.

Something isn't right. I wish my brother would open his eyes. He wasn't ready to have a kid seventeen years ago and now all his issues are starting to shine through in Ronnie.

They think they can just pray for him and send him to prayer camps, but I see it. I see Ronnie needs serious help. I see he needs people here in the community to be your hands and feet. But they won't let me get close to him because Mom and Dad told them fantastic lies about me. And now I'm the only one that wants to speak the truth about what's really happening. Where this is all headed if something isn't done.

Source: Wesley Quino, 39

DAY: FRIDAY, JANUARY 22
TIME: 5:32 P.M.
LOCATION: BARNES DRIVEWAY

Okay, time to do the *Driving Miss Daisy* act. Good thing I like Harriett. I could post a video of our situation and it would go viral in no time. Probably get some racial pity from the internet too. She has a good heart, though. Or at least looks past the irony of me being her fake part-time caretaker. We should make a YouTube channel. Harriett and Harrison Take the Road. Nah. Harrison Takes the Road … and Harriett's There Too. Her Christmas treats make it worth it, though. I wonder if she knows I let her win in SKIP-BO.

I'll miss her whenever she does give up her firm grip on life. I'll need to find another old White lady to drive around.

Source: Harrison Barnes, 32

DAY: SATURDAY, JANUARY 23
TIME: 12:08 A.M.
LOCATION: SWEETIE'S TAVERN PARKING LOT

Here we go! Quick pray and play before we head home. God, keep our breath alcohol-free and keep the fuzz asleep tonight.

Source: Dennis Shanty, 22

Time: 12:09 A.M.
Location: Sweetie's Tavern Parking Lot

Dear Heavenly Father, I apologize for the heathenness of this fool next to me. I don't want to die tonight; I have good brunch plans tomorrow. So please help us get home safe.

Source: Cooper Knucks, 21

Day: Sunday, January 24
Time: 10:21 A.M.
Location: New Haven Youth Room

If I'm gonna be here against my will, at least let that cute boy show up or somethin'.
    I'll hallelujah to that.

Source: Theresa Franklin, 16

Day: Monday, January 25
Time: 4:14 P.M.
Location: Branch Backyard

Puhhllleeeease please please please please please please tell my parents to let me keep this dog I just found. It's amazing and cute and funny and harmless and only smells a little but I will take care of him … or her … oh, no, yeah, her, and I'll pick up her poop and make sure she doesn't pee in the house and do everything right and pleeeeeease convince my parents.

Source: Miles Branch, 9

Day: Tuesday, January 26
Time: 6:13 a.m.
Location: Crooked Heights High School Weight Room

Y'all better pray to God today! I can tell y'all ain't ready. Matter fact, I got y'all just 'cause I can tell you need it: Lord, oh, sweet, sweet, Lord, you know as much as I do that these young boys, and girl, are not ready for the sweat today. They still got the sleep in their eyes, Lord! Wake them up! Wake up their souls! Because I'm going to take them today. Oh, yes, Lord, their souls will be mine if you do not get them ready. You better give them strength, you better give them endurance, you better give them everything you got, because I'm gonna test it all today. Bless this space! And bless their sweat!

And all the sleepyheads said?

Amen.

ALL OF THE SLEEPYHEADS SAID?

AMEN!

Source: Oliver Pernell, 47

Day: Wednesday, January 27
Time: 9:58 a.m.
Location: Brookdale and Shine Street ATM

Here we go, God. Do some miracles like I know you can. Just throw another zero in there. No one will notice. Just a little secret between you and me.

Source: Mick Taylen, 29

DAY: THURSDAY, JANUARY 28
TIME: 12:14 P.M.
LOCATION: ROSE MOUND MIDDLE SCHOOL CAFETERIA

Jesus, thanks for extra chicken nuggets on Thursdays. And thanks for lunch with my friend.

That's what I was gonna say.

Well, you can pray for your lunch too.

But we pray together on Thursdays, that's what we said we were gonna do.

Fine. Say something.

Umm, yeah, thanks for great chicken nuggets on Thursdays.

I already said that.

I know, but I wasn't ready to start praying yet. You can't rush me like that.

Well, hurry up and say something. I'm hungry.

Thanks for the good grades on my test today too, God.

This is supposed to be about lunch. You need to bless our food.

I can pray what I want.

Whatever. Are you done?

Hold on, I also want to say thanks for lunch with my friend.

Nice. Amen.

Amen.

Source: Bryce Loon, 13, and Louis Dander, 13

DAY: FRIDAY, JANUARY 29
TIME: 4:58 P.M.
LOCATION: CAMDEN FIRST BANK

Thank the Lord for another five o'clock on Friday! I hope y'all have a great weekend and that God gives me a bunch of money so y'all won't see me on Monday. Just kidding, you know I care deeply about my job, Sophia. But also, why not ask God to do something great, ya know? Peace.

Source: Quincy Morton, 32

DAY: SATURDAY, JANUARY 30
TIME: 7:17 P.M.
LOCATION: LANSING LIVING ROOM

Thank you for another week to be your servant, Lord. I love the great sleep I've been getting this week. That's been a pleasant surprise. Please look over my family as they travel for vacation next week. Help my grandsons get better manners. They will not get great wives acting like that. Help our church continue to touch people in the community and please let me be a part of spreading the Good News as long as you keep putting breath in my lungs. Lastly, of course, please continue to look after Maleek as he grows up into a young man. I know he won't say it, but there is a lot on his shoulders right now.
    Amen.

Source: Gigi Lansing, 82

Day: Sunday, January 31
TIME: 8:03 P.M.
LOCATION: NEW HAVEN BREAKOUT ROOM

Lord, please give me the courage to lead the group this year. I want this group to do for the broken people in our church what you did for me. I want to show them there is another way. I want to show them you are the way through anything.

Source: Chelsea Elling, 58

DAY: MONDAY, FEBRUARY 1
TIME: 7:14 A.M.
LOCATION: SAUDINER HALF BATH

Help my little brother. Help him be exactly who he is supposed to be. I've known he's different since he started talking, but that didn't keep me from watching over him. I don't know how or what to say to him. But I hope he knows I'll love him no matter who he loves.

Source: Everett Saudiner, 27

DAY: TUESDAY, FEBRUARY 2
TIME: 1:27 P.M.
LOCATION: QUIKTRIP

Yoooooooooo you see what Coach just sent everyone?
What?
Practice canceled today.
God's looking out for us.
Hallelujah and amen to that.

Source: Yaz Azure, 19, and Royce Smith, 18

Day: Wednesday, February 3
Time: 6:52 a.m.
Location: Zen Home Office

Thank you for the time to spend with you today, God. Thank you for this space and freedom to worship you. Thank you for the health of my wife and my beautiful babies. Please help me be the best father I can be for them. Help me learn every day and walk humbly in your footsteps as our great Father.

Please speak through me tonight, like you do every Wednesday, to reach these young boys and girls coming to meet you. Help me pull them closer to you and open their hearts to your power. I know I can do very little, but it's a good thing you can do a lot with a little.

Help me waste not a single opportunity with these kids as I know each day that goes by is another day for them to get distracted by the things of this world. Let me speak with confidence and passion in your name.

Amen.

Source: Wayne Zen, 35

CHAPTER TWO
The Parking Lot

It's the first thing you notice, or don't, depending on the situation. I've never been in a parking lot that was crappy and felt relieved about it. People want to know they are leaving their car in a place that is cared for. Watched over. Loved on a little. Good thing I love it a lot. The fact they didn't ask about the lot the first few months told me all I need to know about the leadership here. Good folks. But still have some learning to do about people. It's always about the people. People don't want to worry about their shoes getting wet from gigantic puddles in the parking lot. People don't want to rush out of church to get out of the parking lot as quickly as possible before it becomes a battleground for escape. A church parking lot is funny that way. It's the first place you get to try to apply the "lesson" the preacher fed that morning. They walk back to their cars and either feel bad because the preacher called out their sin today or feel a little smug as they try to help their partner deal with the difficult, but necessary, words the preacher shared *just for them* today. I'm sure sometimes the lessons never go beyond this parking lot. People put on their Jesus caps when they pull in and toss them off quickly as they pull out and race toward Chili's. We all need our baby back ribs.

The church parking lot is like a car wash in that way. People come in desperately needing a cleanse and drive out feeling sparkly from the day's word. Folks can't stay clean, though. The dirt is relentless. The bugs are suicidal. So here they are every Sunday driving in and driving out and driving in and driving out. It may be blasphemy for me to think this as a sanitation professional, but maybe there's a thing as too much cleaning? All that pressure washing and scrubbing and brushing and soaping. It has to start to lose its effect eventually. The routine will start to leave a few specks here and there. Only natural. Maybe they notice and they turn the soap up next time. Spend a few more minutes getting squeaky clean. But what about the time after that? And the one after that? The commitment to the cleanse is the difficult part. Much easier to let those few specks become a part of the car for good. No one will notice after a few months anyway. They add character, as my dad used to say. Character spots. Everyone has them. Some have a few more than others. Don't let them get out of control, or become too obvious, and no one will know the better.

I see them. I see all the spots. This parking lot has many spots. But what's one man to do? A repaint is costly, and not church budget approved. A touch-up on the lines? *Maybe*, Marcus says. I know what that means. I can tell he thinks I'm crazy for putting so much effort into an area of the church people spend the least amount of time in, but he doesn't see the importance of it like I do. Sure, it's the first impression which always earns the big show. But it's also the last one, the last moment where these people decide if they will come back or start searching for another church with a more welcoming entrance. After all, it's the cast of the lot.

Day: Thursday, February 4
Time: 3:52 p.m.
Location: Rose Mound Middle School Bus Parking Lot

Okay now, Lord, now this is on you now. Now you know I know you know I know these kids don't mean nothing by what they say. It's no secret my patience has been tested over the years and I have always prevailed over my anger through your grace and calming nature and the occasional sleeping pill. But right now, this time right now, with these kids right here right now, do not let them test me today. My ears are too cold and my toes are too sweaty for much more of the debauchery. Now is the time to perform a miracle and give the kids the spirit of stillness you are always talking about. Let their legs be still and their mouths be quiet. Just—just for right now.

Source: Alfred Santorin, 58

Day: Friday, February 5
Time: 8:02 p.m.
Location: Evergreen Wild Casino Bar

A little gambling never hurt nobody. And nobody here knows I'm a pastor's wife anyway. I'm only trying to double the tithe; you know that God.

Source: Emory Garland, 47

DAY: SATURDAY, FEBRUARY 6
TIME: 2:27 P.M.
LOCATION: SALTWATER HALL B MACKENZIE COLLEGE ROOM 216

God ... is that how you start? I'm not sure. Some guy with bad breath handed me this Bible in the café, and for some reason, I didn't want to throw it away like the last few—sorry about that. I honestly don't know why I'm doing this—or if I'm doing this right—but I do feel like something is missing in me ... that's what you fix, right? Fill people with tongues or something? Or is that Muslims? I don't know ... I'm gonna go.

See you later ... eh, amen. Right? Amen?

Source: Kamden Upstin, 18

DAY: SUNDAY, FEBRUARY 7
TIME: 8:42 A.M.
LOCATION: NEW HAVEN AUDITORIUM

Thank you, Jesus, for facial hair. He just looks wiser with it up there. I've tried to tell him for years now.

Source: Emory Garland, 47

DAY: MONDAY, FEBRUARY 8
TIME: 7:09 A.M.
LOCATION: FAULKNER KITCHEN

Thanks for breakfast and all, God. But you didn't help me find all the answers on the back of the box. I need those answers. And Mommy looked sad this morning. Please help Mommy not be sad.

Source: Izzy Faulkner, 6

DAY: TUESDAY, FEBRUARY 9
TIME: 10:48 P.M.
LOCATION: JOYCE BEDROOM

Pray, pray, pray. Say, say, say. Saying my prayers and praying my sayers. Have to say something or else I'll be in trouble when my parents ask. So I'm here now pray, pray, praying. Even though I never hear anything from you, God, I'll keep saying something because that's what I'm supposed to do. Saying and praying. Praying and saying. Okay, time's about up. Making the parents happy. Hear from you later, but probably not because I never hear from you.

Source: Zehare Joyce, 15

DAY: WEDNESDAY, FEBRUARY 10
TIME: 8:13 A.M.
LOCATION: FORT MIND HIGH SCHOOL CLASSROOM 313

Okay, Big Bro, I know I said this last time, and, sure, the time before that too, but this time I'm with it: help me pass this test and I got you. I'll go to church. I'll tell my little brother to go to church. I won't cuss ... for at least a few weeks. I'll stop watching po—well, you know, I'll just be better. I'm not asking for much, just something reasonable, like an 82 would be clutch. 82 and I got you.

Source: Xavier Balden, 16

Day: Thursday, February 11
Time: 2:44 P.M.
Location: Target Parking Lot

MAY GAWD HAVE MERCY ON YOUR SOUL! MAY HE FIND FORGIVENESS FOR YOUR MANY TRESPASSES! I PRAY THAT YOU FIND HIM BEFORE THE DAY COMES. YOU KNOW THE DAY ... THE DAY IS APPROACHING AND YOU WILL NOT BE READY! I CAN ONLY PRAY FOR SO MANY LOST SOULS, DON'T LET YOURS BE THE ONE I FORGET! I'M NOT PERFECT. NO ONE IS! BUT AT LEAST MY EYES ARE OPEN AND I KNOW THE END-TIMES ARE NEAR! COME! COME ONE, COME ALL! SEEK THE TRUTH YOU MUST! COME REPENT OF YOUR SINS AND SAVE YOURSELVES WHILE YOU CAN. THE DAY IS COMING!

Source: Verl Muncy, 62

Day: Friday, February 12
Time: 7:43 A.M.
Location: Denny's Parking Lot

Allllllright now, God, it's been a minute for this old cat. I know my knees and my hips don't work like they used to, but I'm sure I still got some charm left. I know she ain't take all that with her when she left me to go hang out with you. How is she doing? She still talkin' all the time? Ahh, well, I'm sure she would want me to be happy and at least have a date or two. I know they'll never replace her, but they might be able to cook better. I'm playin' ... I miss that pecan pie every day. Oh well, time to see if this old fox still got it. Miss you always, my Betty Bee.

Source: Prentice Truth, 77

Day: Saturday, February 13
Time: 6:42 a.m.
Location: Rick-Mobile

Father, as always, we thank you for these day trips we have with each other. I selfishly thank you for blinding this beautiful woman for seventeen years and pray that you never open her eyes and see how much better she could be doing. We pray for open roads, green lights, and clear skies.

Okay, now you can talk to God about how great I am.

Hmm. I think I'm good. God is good and I didn't hear any lies in there.

Seventeen years later and I can't get a bone. Classic.

Amen to that. Let's get this Rick-Mobile in action.

Source: Tanner Rick, 39, and Willow Rick, 43

Day: Sunday, February 14
Time: 3:33 p.m.
Location: Macary Park Bathroom

I'm here still waiting to be saved, God. I'm sure you have forgotten about me by now. You must have—there's no way you still hear me. I did everything right. I always stayed out of trouble. I always went to church growing up. That was years ago now, but all those hours were supposed to count for something. I can't live like this much longer ....

Source: Ulises Zind, 41

Day: Tuesday, February 16
Time: 5:05 p.m.
Location: Branch Backyard

God, thanks for making the last three "test weeks" go great. I can't believe I taught her to only pee outside ... after those first few accidents, of course. Since then, I've killed it. Put my parents in a good mood this weekend when they make the final decision. I have a good feeling about it, but I know you can give them that little extra push. There's no way they could put Juniper out in the cold in the winter! There's no way ....

Source: Miles Branch, 9

Day: Wednesday, February 17
Time: 10:49 p.m.
Location: Haranna Bedroom

How long is long enough, Father?

It's been two years and I feel like I'm the only one trying to push us forward. I'm trying to get us up and over the mountain that our mom's death created, but I can't go alone. My dad ... well, that's Dad. I'll worry about him next. My little brother needs to get it together—like, now. I miss her just as much as he does, but we both know she wouldn't let him stay in this slump he's in. At least let him slump somewhere else. My patience and hospitality are starting to run thin.

Please shake them up. Shake them awake.

Source: Estella Haranna, 39

DAY: FRIDAY, FEBRUARY 19
TIME: 6:07 P.M.
LOCATION: METZEN BATHROOM

I'm too tired to be the peacekeeper between Kenny and Hauz this year. Please help them take the next step this year, even if it's the tiniest baby step, I still want to see a step. Some sort of positive movement between them. Help them see the good in the other. Help them see the good I see in them both.

If nothing else, give me a few more moments of silence this year.

Source: Penelope Metzen, 39

DAY: SATURDAY, FEBRUARY 20
TIME: 10:18 A.M.
LOCATION: CRIMSON PARK TRAIL

I'm sorry, God. This was not a good week. I'm all over the place. I'm impatient. I'm judgy. I'm quickly irritated. I know it's starting to rub off on my students too. Salem and the rest of my learners don't need to see my ugly side like that.

Most of all, I'm sorry I haven't been coming to you first with everything. You've been getting a lot of my scraps when you should be getting my first. I know that. This wasn't the start to the year I wanted, but I know you can and you will turn it around. I just need to get out of your way.

Source: Angel Zombuka, 28

DAY: SUNDAY, FEBRUARY 21
TIME: 4:01 P.M.
LOCATION: BRANCH GARAGE

LET'S GOOOOOO! I knew you had my back! I never doubted it for a second. I'm never going to do anything wrong with Juniper. She is going to be the best dog we have ever had. Well, she's the first dog we ever had, but I know she's going to be the best too. Just look at her. She looks so happy. I don't care that some people think she's ugly. She's adorable to me. You're the best, God.

Source: Miles Branch, 9

DAY: MONDAY, FEBRUARY 22
TIME: 10:13 P.M.
LOCATION: CURTIS BEDROOM

Happy Monday, Lord. We've been taking it easy today ... besides thinking about how much we believe in you to give us a baby this year.
    Very subtle.
    I'm just putting yesterday's message into practice and not limiting God to our "small" prayers. He made you and me and to be here at this time and bring a beautiful life into this world ... I can feel it ....
    Preach, preacher ....
    I'm trying. Lord, help us continue to be faithful to you in all ways and to not diminish how great you are. You are bigger than anything we could bring to you, including this future baby, and let us find comfort in that. Thank you for each day to live for you and thank you for the support of our friends and family as we try to squeeze one more into your kingdom.
    And all the present, and future, Curtis clan said Amen.

Source: Tricia Curtis, 31, and Graham Curtis, 29

DAY: WEDNESDAY, FEBRUARY 24
TIME: 12:09 P.M.
LOCATION: HAMMY'S DRIVE-THRU

Hey, Pops. Can I call you Pops? Doesn't feel right, but I'll go with it for now. Just me again, asking you to make this little man like me. I call him "man" because he has been acting like he's the man of the house. Sure, I get it, I'm some random dude off the streets moving into the house who forgets his socks in the living room. He probably imagines this is an extended sleepover I'm having with his mom. I want to respect his space. Help me with that. But help him understand I'm assisting with the bills now, and his lunch money, so he can at least act like I deserve some sort of authority. A smidge of respect is all I want. A smidge ...

Source: Kenny Sturgiss, 37

DAY: THURSDAY, FEBRUARY 25
TIME: 9:27 A.M.
LOCATION: ARMUN HOME OFFICE (CLOSET)

Good morning, God. Can you hear me okay? Well, of course I can walk through the strengths I will bring to the team.

First, I'm people focused. I know nothing gets done without understanding the needs of the team and then fulfilling those needs in the most effective and efficient ways possible.

Next, my passion. This may sound cheesy, but I don't have any quit in me. And when joining a start-up, I've often seen that the passion of the team members can be the secret sauce that keeps the engine going when things seem to be breaking down.

Lastly, some other third thing that I'll pull out of my behind ... tuhhh ... okay, I'll work on that one.

Would you hire me, God? Because you might be the last one left. Please let this be the beginning of the end of this job search.

Source: Yasmine Armun, 24

DAY: FRIDAY, FEBRUARY 26
TIME: 9:42 P.M.
LOCATION: TANGER ROAD EMBASSY SUITES ELEVATOR

This is part of it. Making myself available and going where these people are. Lord, please help Jessica overcome her addiction. I know her life can be so much more than this cycle she is caught in. Give her courage and strength to seek help and believe in herself to defeat its grip on her life.

Help me be a support beam for her right now. To listen and love first. To act unselfishly. And believe in your power to transform lives.

Amen.

Source: Chelsea Elling, 58

DAY: SATURDAY, FEBRUARY 27
TIME: 3:44 P.M.
LOCATION: SOUTHWEST FLIGHT 8672 ROW 22 SEAT C

You know the drill ... please give our pilots strength and wisdom as we take off today. Let there be no clouds, no birds, nothing up there today, God. Make this flight as smooth as possible. No bumpies. No turbulence. And no crying babies.

Really, if you want to knock me out right now and wake me up when I get to the hotel, I'd be fine with that. Or at least let them provide the good pretzels this time around.

Source: Saul Welter, 54

DAY: SUNDAY, FEBRUARY 28
TIME: 5:42 A.M.
LOCATION: VERDANA BATHROOM

Two months in and nothing has changed. I'm doing all the little things right. I'm eating right. I'm sleeping enough. I'm walking and walking and walking—all I do is walk. Why won't you help me with this, Lord? Why won't you help me overcome this? This can't be how I'm supposed to look. This can't be how you want me to look. I don't understand.

Why won't you help me with this?

Source: Bri Verdana, 29

DAY: MONDAY, MARCH 1
TIME: 8:03 A.M.
LOCATION: ROSE MOUND MIDDLE SCHOOL CAFETERIA

You musta not heard me the first time, but "Dr. Sturgiss," as he likes to call himself, really *really* needs to chill out. Why does he think he needs to be in my room? It's my room! Not even my mom goes in there and now this local joker with a lame corporate job wants to help me *organize*. What does that even mean?

He can stay in his space. I'll stay in mine, and I'll allow him to continue living in *my* house. I don't want to get ugly with him, but he's pushing me.

Source: Hauz Metzen, 14

DAY: TUESDAY, MARCH 2
TIME: 11:11 A.M.
LOCATION: KING$ DREAM STUDIO

God, please bless this time we have today in the studio. Help us clear our minds of distractions and open them up for the creative juice. Speak and write through us and help us spread your truth to ears all over the state ... and then the world.

Source: Booker Naheem, 21

DAY: WEDNESDAY, MARCH 3
TIME: 4:42 P.M.
LOCATION: GARLAND HOME OFFICE

Jesus, please help this storm be bad tonight so church stuff is canceled and I don't have to go sit around and act like I want to be there.

Source: Jonah Garland, 15

Day: Thursday, March 4
Time: 6:31 a.m.
Location: Garland Home Office

Sometimes I wish I married a doctor. Sorry, I don't mean that. Dr. Byrdwood probably has a great pocketbook, but Marcus has a great heart. My mom was so happy when I told her Marcus was in ministry school, but my dad knew what that meant. He saw the dollar signs start to fade away as we got more serious. He never said anything, though. Bless his heart. I hope you're doing good up there, Daddy.

These numbers just get harder to make work each year. The church is alive and well, but we won't be if we keep heading in this direction.

Make these numbers make sense, God.

Source: Emory Garland, 47

Day: Saturday, March 6
Time: 2:27 p.m.
Location: Concord Convention Center Locker Room

Here we go, God. This is it. You've been with us the entire season, through this magical run. Now we come to give you praise for this opportunity to finish how we want. Win or lose, we know you will be with us.

Win ...

Win or lose, we know we are worthy of your guidance.

Win ...

Win or win, we know we are lucky to be here right now with each other.

That's better.

Help us play fast, safe, and tough. And for the last time this season—in your name we play.

Source: Layla Sacron, 17

Day: Sunday, March 7
Time: 10:42 a.m.
Location: New Haven Auditorium

Wow. I can't believe it's over. I can't believe high school is almost over. I don't feel ready, God. Everything seems to be happening really fast. We literally lost the championship yesterday, and today it's "time to start thinking about the future." Thanks for all that patience, Mom. How did Sherise miss that shot? How did we forget we had another time-out? How did I step out-of-bounds? That pissed me off. Mm-hmm. Sorry sorry sorry. That was yesterday and today is today. Help me live for you today, and I'll let you figure out my future. Good luck with that.

Source: Layla Sacron, 17

CHAPTER THREE
The Nursery

They were never for me. All the smells. All the responsibilities. All the helplessness. I hate to imagine myself as a baby. Relying on other people to take care of me. Not for me. Grandma did say I was one of the quickest children she ever saw learn how to get into the fridge. If I can do it myself, then I don't have to rely on others, and if I don't have to rely on others then I won't be disappointed by others. I'd rather look in the mirror than look through a baby monitor. That's just me, though. Luckily, I'm the minority. If there were too many me's in the world, there wouldn't be any me's in the world. I get it, so I get with it. The babies matter. Making the babies comfortable matters. Making the babies safe matters the most. I've seen pictures of my old crib, and it wouldn't pass the legal code for the things we are putting in this place. Some of these look like rocket ships. I can put together about anything, but these might give me a run for my money. You think they would make these as easy as possible for all the dummies out there having babies, but maybe it's made to be a wake-up call. Like, hey Mom and Dad, if you can't put this together you shouldn't be multiplying. That's one thing I know for certain: if a baby doesn't wake you up to the real world, then you might be asleep forever. Every person has minimum two people inside of them—their prebaby self and postbaby self. I assumed I would get along with everyone's prebaby self more than the post based on my sensibilities, but as I've gotten older, I've been pleasantly surprised by some folks. Some people get the ignorant knocked out of them, which we all need from time to time. Others get scared straight by long stays at the hospital. A few lose all their sense of fun, which sucks, but lack of sleep and baby poo will do that to you. But most are just *consumed*. Every second of every day and every decision is consumed by these little things who can't say thank you. Even if they wanted to it would come out as spittle probably. Then I come in and clean it up from the floors. And the sink. And the ceiling. And everything in between. An endless ball of mess. It's impressive honestly. My greatest adversaries in this entire building are the most adorable ones at the same time.

I wonder if God gets tired of wiping the bum of all his children? I didn't sign up to do it once, but he is constantly accepting applications for daddy duty. Seems a little too eager stepfatherish for me, but I get it, he can perform miracles and all that. The ultimate Bring Your Parent to School Day trump card. If I was in his shoes, I'd be picky about who's getting into the family and not, because some of these people are the worst child-adults I've ever witnessed. They're spoiled teenagers upset about not going where they want on vacation instead of appreciating they're going on vacation at all. They should be silent in the back of the minivan and happy the family can afford a road trip. Just as messy in the back seat as their real kids are in my nursery. There shouldn't be crumbs on the ceiling. I probably shouldn't complain. I'm only seeing the aftermath of whatever went down when the battle was live in here. Bless those baby lovers. Those are the real miracle workers.

DAY: MONDAY, MARCH 8
TIME: 2:02 A.M.
LOCATION: SILENT NIGHT COFFEE SHOP

I can't believe it's come to this, God. I don't know what to do anymore. Please help me escape this man. I hate the choice you've brought me to. Those kids in the nursery at church fill me up more than they will ever know, but I have to worry about my own baby first and foremost. I fear for the safety of my child and myself. Please help him just … disappear. Help him find someone else to terrorize. Help him find another woman. I don't care. Remove him from my life.

Source: Beiba Palmandi, 45

DAY: TUESDAY, MARCH 9
TIME: 9:02 P.M.
LOCATION: GRANT BEDROOM

Jesus, I know you don't want these people coming into our country. Give us the power to keep them out. Protect our people at the border. Protect our servicemen. Keep them safe from all of these reckless people who think they know better than our government. Who think they know better than you! For all I care, you can remove them all from our streets.

Thank you for the freedoms you provide us and let no one stand against us.

Source: Austin Grant, 57

Day: Thursday, March 11
Time: 5:15 p.m.
Location: Tops and Bickles Band Practice (Fermington Garage)

Let us melt some faces at the festival this weekend, Jesus.
    Amen. And one, two, three!

Source: Trevor Fermington, 17

Day: Friday, March 12
Time: 11:32 p.m.
Location: Armun Home Office (Closet)

Okay. It's been over two weeks. Should I hit them with another "just checking in" email? A girl's gotta know. A girl's gotta eat. Why is this all so complicated, God? I know they aren't purposefully wasting my time by not letting me know where I am in the process, but maybe coincidentally doing it? Either way, time is ticking ... but good thing you are beyond space and time and can perform miraculous things like getting people jobs they are overqualified for but still are always somehow underqualified to get the max pay but would still love that pay because they need to be able to feed themselves but more importantly feed their cat who is going to start nibbling on them if they don't come home with the bacon soon.
    Fine, I'll be patient and be faithful or whatever.
    Amen.

Source: Yasmine Armun, 24

DAY: SATURDAY, MARCH 13
TIME: 7:48 A.M.
LOCATION: SALTWATER HALL B MACKENZIE COLLEGE ROOM 216

I'm tired. This is me doing what that preacher on YouTube said to do and making time for you in my mornings. Are you a morning person? Is this when you hear prayers better or something? He also said to start reading something from this old book each day but where am I supposed to start? This seems like a lot. Maybe I'll just close my eyes for a few more seconds to get inspired to read ....

Source: Kamden Upstin, 18

DAY: SUNDAY, MARCH 14
TIME: 9:59 A.M.
LOCATION: NEW HAVEN KIDS ROOM

Jesus, we thank you for letting us come to church this morning. For helping us learn. And for giving us time to play as well. We thank you for great teachers like Mrs. A. and Honey.
    Amen—oh, we thank you for the church doughnuts as well.
    Amen.

Source: Izzy Faulkner, 6

DAY: MONDAY, MARCH 15
TIME: 6:22 A.M.
LOCATION: CROOKED HEIGHTS HIGH SCHOOL TRACK

Oh, Jesus! Jesus help these kids today! They too sleepy! Y'all don't know about the Ides of March, huh? They ain't teaching y'all anything in that school? Good thing I'm the professor this morning. Just because God told me to be merciful on this heavenly, crisp morning, if any one of you can name what famous play speaks on the Ides of March I'll take it easy on you poor souls. Anyone? Anyone feeling brave today?

Uh, "Hamilton"?

Hamilton? Oh hell nah, just for that get on the curve right now! *Hamilton?* They ain't teaching y'all squat! They need to start paying me for this knowledge I'm trying to share. Stretching is over. I said get on the curve! Eight hundreds!

Source: Oliver Pernell, 47

DAY: WEDNESDAY, MARCH 17
TIME: 12:33 P.M.
LOCATION: SAMANTHA'S SOUPS AND SAMMIES EATERY

Please give my business wings this year, God. I need it to take off. For me. I'm tired of telling my husband that we're "just around the corner" from success. He would never say anything to me about it, but he doesn't need to. I know it's now or never.

Source: Veronica Chaucer, 36

DAY: THURSDAY, MARCH 18
TIME: 12:02 A.M.
LOCATION: SAUDINER BEDROOM

I don't want this. I don't want any of this. I know this isn't me. I can't be feeling this way. I'm a Christian. I know I am. I am a man of God. I don't like other men.

Remove these thoughts from my head, God. Please.

Source: Dustin Saudiner, 20

Day: Friday, March 19
Time: 5:05 p.m.
Location: Camden First Bank

Do ya happy dance! Do ya happy dance! Praise Jesus! Praise Jesus!
I'm leaving! I'm leaving! It's the weekend! It's the weekend!
  Amen! Amen!

Source: Quincy Morton, 32

Day: Saturday, March 20
Time: 9:14 a.m.
Location: Hanoi Backyard

Very disappointing, Mr. Christ. We had a deal: I'm a good kid, you
tell my parents to let me watch cartoons on Saturday morning.

  Now, look at me, out here ... outside ... being forced to play.
Play is for babies. I'm an entire seven-year-old. Seven-year-olds
watch cartoons. We need to figure this whole thing out. This will
not work for the summer. Much too hot.

Source: Victor Hanoi, 7

Day: Sunday, March 21
Time: 6:13 p.m.
Location: Harolds Dining Room

Jesus, help this boy, he has lost his damn mind. I did not teach him to cook and eat like that. That must come from his father.

Come on, Ma, it's not that—

I said, Jesus, have mercy on my taste buds! Remove this boy from his sin so he can see clearly in the kitchen.

Now you're doing too much—

Jesus!

Source: Umi Harolds, 57

Day: Monday, March 22
Time: 8:39 p.m.
Location: Faulkner Bedroom

What were my parents whispering about earlier today? They almost sounded ... scared. It was probably about Izzy. I know they don't try to favor her around me, but I get it. She's the baby. I know the rest of my life will center around making her happy. It is nice when they forget about me every now and then—especially when I do something stupid. I just can't help myself. All the stupid things are fun.

Whatever they were talking about, I pray it's not a big deal.

Source: Salem Faulkner, 14

Day: Tuesday, March 23
Time: 7:30 p.m.
Location: New Haven Auditorium Prayer Night

Heavenly Father,

Please bring my son, Zehare, into your arms. I can feel him fighting his father and me and running away from you. I don't know what to do. We make him come to all the church activities. We make him memorize scripture. We make him volunteer with us. Nothing seems to work. I don't want to beat the Bible into him, but he is so stubborn. He believes he can live life without you, without anyone. If only he knew what we went through to have him. Speak into his heart, Lord. Reveal yourself to him.

Amen.

Source: Helena Joyce, 40

Day: Wednesday, March 24
Time: 8:42 a.m.
Location: Wallard Driveway

Huh. Where is she at? She knows I don't like to sit out here and wait. This neighborhood is too nice for a brother just to chill in the driveway like this.

Maybe she finally didn't wake up today. She has started to move a little slower. I would hate that, for me to be the one to find her all cold. Who do you call? 911? Like, *this old lady dead, y'all.* Or—wow, she was just putting on her "nice" wig.

Thanks for another day of Lady Wallard, God.

Source: Harrison Barnes, 32

DAY: THURSDAY, MARCH 25
TIME: 8:01 A.M.
LOCATION: RUDY'S PHARMACY

Father, please help this business do what it was supposed to do when I started. It was supposed to help people. It was supposed to be a place where I could help people live better lives. A place for people to find relief and continue to do things that make life worth living. Now I feel like everything I'm forced to do makes life unaffordable for these people. I hate being forced to compete, if I can call it that, with "big pharma" just to provide for my family. There has to be a better way to help these people. Help me find that ....

Source: Rudy Norman, 38

DAY: FRIDAY, MARCH 26
TIME: 7:04 P.M.
LOCATION: GARLAND ROOF

Wow. Thanks for this beautiful scene. For this job. For this air.
    You coming down, Benny? Sun's going down, we gotta get back to the office.
    Yeah, I'm just appreciatin' God's handiwork. Check out this sky.
    You'll see another one like it in three weeks. C'mon.
    Probably. But I have this one now. If God's givin' out a freebie, why not accept?

Source: Benny Furtan, 22

DAY: SATURDAY, MARCH 27
TIME: 5:45 A.M.
LOCATION: MINTERSON COUNTY POLICE STATION

Thank you for another day to protect my family and my community. Thank you for the opportunity to wear this badge. Let me wear it with pride to honor those before me and create the *right* example for those after me. Help me bring my community together in these difficult times. And keep all my brothers and sisters in the force safe.

Source: Danielle Grainger, 33

DAY: MONDAY, MARCH 29
TIME: 11:48 P.M.
LOCATION: HARANNA LIVING ROOM

Thank you for giving me another day to live and love for you, God. Thanks for that interview last week. And thanks for another good week of job applications. Everything has been great lately—except for my sister. Help her ... loosen up? I don't know what it is, I know she thinks I'm not trying to get back right after Mom died, but some of us don't have the switch like she does. She puts too much pressure on herself too. That's it: help her find the freedom to breathe and take a seat sometimes. She can take a break from trying to run me and Dad back into shape.
    Amen.

Source: Leo Haranna, 37

DAY: TUESDAY, MARCH 30
TIME: 4:44 P.M.
LOCATION: CURTIS MASTER BATH

This is me being as committed with the prayers as possible—please, please give us a baby this year. I know I want this bad, but she feels like she *needs* this. Honestly, it probably isn't healthy. I don't know why it has become the focus of our relationship like this ... well, I do, I guess. Once she hit thirty something changed. I think she is afraid time is running out. I wish she would stop reading every fertility article out there.

Just a sign, just something moving us in the right direction. Each new turn of the calendar is starting to bring her down. I can feel it. I know your plans are bigger than ours, but it would be great if we could get on the same page on this one. For her. For me. For us.

Source: Graham Curtis, 29

DAY: WEDNESDAY, MARCH 31
TIME: 1:14 P.M.
LOCATION: SAUDINER HALF BATH

Should I approach him about it? I don't want to make him uncomfortable. But he is clearly living a life that's uncomfortable for him now. I want him to feel as free as you want him to be, God. My parents might never get it. But they grew up in a different time. In a different church.

Give me the words to say and the courage to say them.

Source: Everett Saudiner, 27

DAY: THURSDAY, APRIL 1
TIME: 6:22 P.M.
LOCATION: GRANT BEDROOM

Don't allow those folks into our schools, God. Keep them and their "theories" away from our kids. That's all nonsense. They just want to teach a different version of history—a fake version. They want to remove everything our forefathers did to create this beautiful country. Don't let them do it. Preserve our nation. Help us squash these false teachings.

Source: Austin Grant, 57

DAY: FRIDAY, APRIL 2
TIME: 5:13 A.M.
LOCATION: WALLARD BEDROOM

Ninety-two. I can't believe I made it another year. I must have great genes, huh, Jesus? Well, thanks for the long life, but I'm about ready to go. All of my friends have been gone for years. The only food I can eat now always comes out looking gray. Who wants gray food? There's nothing good on TV. I've made it through two husbands and all these other guys are just a bunch of old farts. I'm tired. And I know Harrison is getting tired of losing to me in cards. He really is too gullible.

Source: Harriett Wallard, 92

DAY: SATURDAY, APRIL 3
TIME: 11:02 A.M.
LOCATION: NINEH GARAGE

I actually have a prayer for you, Oh Mighty One, who only seems to come up in conversation around this time of year and Christmas. I'd love it if my overly friendly neighbor Jeremiah didn't ask me to come to church with him or ask me about my "relationship" with you this week. I know he's trying to be a good Christian, whatever that means, but I'm over the routine ... and the effort. How many years of me blowing him off does it take for him to stop inviting me? I'm still on your team; I just don't feel the need to share it on social media or join some community group that is going to ask for my money. I like my private life and occasional chat with you. It works for me.

Source: Jamison Nineh, 35

DAY: MONDAY, APRIL 5
TIME: 7:13 A.M.
LOCATION: SILENT NIGHT COFFEE SHOP DRIVE-THRU

Sometimes I forget that you want me to be present at my real job too. But this job only pays the bills. Helping broken people fills me up. Give me the energy to be great at both.

Source: Chelsea Elling, 58

Day: Tuesday, April 6
Time: 8:26 p.m.
Location: Byrd Street Guitars and Things

Please help this week go by fast. This is one of the worst weeks of the year to be a pastor's kid. My friends actually expect me to invite them to church or want me to pray for them or something ... it sucks. Let's fast-forward to next week.

Source: Jonah Garland, 15

Day: Wednesday, April 7
Time: 7:41 p.m.
Location: Silver Stone Business Complex

Okay, I loooove the quick work on this one, Lord! We haven't seen numbers like this since we first started. This is exactly what we needed. I feel like I can breathe again. Keith is going to be so proud of me.

Source: Veronica Chaucer, 36

Day: Thursday, April 8
Time: 11:47 p.m.
Location: King$ Dream Studio

Yeah, this is it. I can feel it. I know you've been leading me to this moment. I know I've followed your will. It's the perfect weekend to pop off on the streams. It's the perfect weekend for you to resurrect my career. Ha. See what I did there? Well, I guess it ain't ever lived in the first place, so more like the perfect weekend for you to remove the stone blocking the world from my music. Ahh, that won't work as a caption. Too long. Whatever. Still. I know you got me in your hand right now. Don't drop me.

Source: Booker Naheem, 21

Day: Friday, April 9
Time: 6:38 a.m.
Location: Many Men Bible Study (Chaucer Kitchen)

As we get closer to the big day, Lord, we look to make time today to reflect on the ultimate sacrifice you made all those years ago. We recognize that it was our sins that nailed you to that cross, but it was through your incredible power that you rose three days later and washed away those very sins. We could never do enough to thank you and pay you back for that, and luckily, that's not what you ask of us. All that you ask is that we receive the gift of an eternal life that you bought with your flesh and blood and understand you are the only way to that eternal life. You did the hard part, the tall task, the big jump, so that all we need to do is open our hearts to you.

Personally, I'm incredibly thankful for that fact. Like most in this room, I make more mistakes than I can count, but with you by my side I know I can always come back correct the next day. Speaking of this room, I'm extremely humbled and grateful for each of these men you have put into my life. They are your hands and feet in this world with me, and I know I don't just speak for myself when I say this group is changing lives.

Let us live for you today and every day.

Amen.

Source: Ian Junith, 32

DAY: SATURDAY, APRIL 10
TIME: 8:58 A.M.
LOCATION: CHAUCER BEDROOM

God, you are amazing. Hearing Ian lead the prayer yesterday … it was just what I needed. It was what we all needed. He has come so far in just a year. Of course, right when I was feeling far from you, you helped me see that everything I'm trying to do with that group is worth it. Even for one person to grow like that makes it all worth it.

Thank you for never giving up on me and never giving up on us. I pray that you keep using that group to do powerful things in your name.

Source: Keith Chaucer, 34

DAY: SUNDAY, APRIL 11
TIME: 10:32 A.M.
LOCATION: NEW HAVEN STAGE

Heavenly Father, we feel you in this place right now. We call on your name and we lift you up. The name above all names. That has never been more true than today. It's true every day, yes, but today we get to celebrate just how powerful your name is, Lord. Your name moves mountains. It stops the sun. Your name breathes life into our lungs. Your name raises the dead!

We come before you today ready to recognize and be thankful that that same power resides within us, Lord. You are our Savior. Our Redeemer. Your sacrifice over two thousand years ago changed history. It changed this world. And it changed each and every one of us.

Thank you for being in this moment with us. Thank you for this time we get to come together and praise you. Open our hearts and minds to receive your word today.

Amen. You may be seated.

Source: Asher Sage, 38

Day: Monday, April 12
Time: 1:02 p.m.
Location: Rudy's Pharmacy Bathroom

This is the last time. I see that now. I know I need help. After this I'll tell Melesia and she'll help me and we'll work together and I'll beat this thing and I won't need these pills to think straight anymore, and I won't need them to get onstage and I won't need them to think straight and I won't need them to be a leader. I'm fine. I can manage. Don't be such a pussy. I can stop whenever I want. This is what they gave to me. How can I be in the wrong? These were supposed to fix me. I don't need to tell anyone. I can help myself. I did it when I was a teenager, and I can do it now. If I did it then I can do it now. If I did it then I can do it now. Last time, last time, last time.

Source: Asher Sage, 38

Day: Tuesday, April 13
Time: 3:34 p.m.
Location: Vintage Spirits Third-Floor Cubicle

This can't be real, God. Are you and he conspiring against me? He's emailing me a list of summer demands? I can't ... I don't ... I need a break. Who does he think he is? How does he even have my email? How do kids know how to email? What. Is. Happening.

Source: Kenny Sturgiss, 37

Day: Wednesday, April 14
Time: 10:13 p.m.
Location: Joyce Bedroom

Lord, please never make me put on that suit again. An Easter Sunday fit? Seriously? Is this 2004? Why can't they let me be? Why am I even talking to you? You probably want me to look and act like them—but I'm not them. I don't care to be a part of the Christian facade and act all holy in public and have the same amount of issues as everyone else in private. That's why I really don't mess with it. It's all so ... fugazi ....

Source: Zehare Joyce, 15

Day: Thursday, April 15
Time: 12:09 p.m.
Location: Rose Mound Middle School Cafeteria

God, I'm sorry for whatever we did to deserve this.

Whoa. Speak for yourself. I didn't do anything ....

Don't lie during prayer like that.

I'm not. My actions had no impact on the lack of chicken nuggets today.

So you're saying I did something wrong then?

That's between you and God.

At least I can ask for forgiveness and maybe he will make sure this doesn't happen again, but if you don't confess then maybe they will never come back.

Fine. I'm sorry, God.

You're sorry for?

Stop worrying about me. Pray for these soft sandwiches so we can eat.

I don't want to pray for them because then we'll have to eat them.

It's better than being hungry.

Is it?

I'm saying "amen" so I can eat.

Are you sure you don't want to confess any sins? I'll forgive you if it was about me.

Amen!

Fine. Amen.

Source: Bryce Loon, 13, and Louis Dander, 13

Day: Friday, April 16
Time: 4:32 p.m.
Location: Armun Home Office (Closet)

Five o'clock on Friday, what a wonderful time. What a freeing time. What a time of bliss. What a time that I wish meant anything to me right now. This whole test of my patience act has gone on long enough, Jesus. I don't know what I'm supposed to be learning from this time. That I'm unemployable? That I don't have a good grasp of my value? I'm feeling worthless. I know that's dumb, and I know I should go to you for my worth, but that's much easier to do when I can afford the gas to drive myself to church each week.

Help me remain committed to this search. Help me stay true to myself and not short sell my benefits. Give me the confidence to get up each day and the belief that the job for me is out there.

Source: Yasmine Armun, 24

Day: Saturday, April 17
Time: 6:42 p.m.
Location: Lansing Living Room

Father, I worry about Maleek. He hasn't called much recently. And when we have spoken his mind seems elsewhere. Make sure he knows I am always here for him. Open his heart to me—and especially to you.

Please help the church continue to grow. Help the church keep up the energy from last week. There is always a big drop-off in activity after Easter. But I know you never stop working on our behalf so help us always be active in your name. Let us continue to fight the good fight.

Oh, and help my flowers bloom better than last spring. I didn't do all that gardening for nothing.

Amen.

Source: Gigi Lansing, 82

Day: Sunday, April 18
Time: 8:06 a.m.
Location: Minterson County Police Station Drunk Tank

Hmm. Okay. Maybe I do have a *slight* problem, God.

Source: Zayn Niro, 44

Day: Monday, April 19
Time: 7:32 a.m.
Location: Fort Mind Weight Room

One month? I'm not ready for this. How did this go by so fast? Can I run it back real quick, God? Honestly, just one more layup line would make me smile. Well, I'll have plenty more layup lines, but not with my girls. I wish we could play this last season over and over again. I wish they could all come to college with me. I hope they're all taking the right next step. What am I saying, I hope I chose the right college or at least the one that chills my parents out.

That's who really needs prayer: my wonderful, stressed, beloved, stressed parents. I've never seen them cry so much over me making breakfast. Like, I'm gonna be back to make toast. It's gonna be okay. I'm only going four hours away. You would think I'm going to school in Boston or something. I am jealous of Cici for that. Good reason to visit now, I guess. Hopefully she makes it last out there. Hmm. I pray I make it last too. I don't want to be that girl who comes crying home to Mom and Dad. Either way, I still can't thank you enough for giving me this chance to continue playing. Help me make the most of it.

Source: Layla Sacron, 17

DAY: TUESDAY, APRIL 20
TIME: 9:47 A.M.
LOCATION: VOLUNTEERS FOR CHEERS LOBBY

I'm nervous, Father. This isn't how I pictured it. I think … I think I thought it would be easier. They say there are all these programs, all these organizations to help us "re-enter" society, but I don't know … I don't know if they can achieve what they want to. It didn't hurt me, but it didn't help me much either. I feel like I'm clawing at every post to get back in, to start my life again, but it's like my life doesn't want me back. Society doesn't want me back. Everyone learned how to live without me, and now there is no space for me. There was space for me in my cell. But there is no space for the new me in society. Only the old me.

Source: Oscar Abbernathy, 61

DAY: WEDNESDAY, APRIL 21
TIME: 10:33 P.M.
LOCATION: VERDANA BATHROOM

Okay okay okay. This is going to be a good step. This step isn't going to scare me anymore. This step is going to start a new movement in my life. Help me step on this scale with confidence in myself, God. Confidence in what I can achieve and who I can become. I'm not going to fear this step anymore.

Source: Bri Verdana, 29

Day: Thursday, April 22
Time: 2:22 p.m.
Location: Macary Park Bench

I want to thank you for helping me get through this winter and into warmer weather, like today, but I'm pretty sure I did all the heavy lifting. That's what's wrong with me. That's why I'm here right now. You always leave me to do the heavy lifting. When I had a home and a life and friends and a family, I built that all up. That was my hard work. And then you let it all fall apart. How could I have stopped any of that? That's not fair. I did my part. Then, when it was your turn to save me, you were nowhere to be found. I gave money. I took my kids to Sunday school. I never hurt my wife. But none of that mattered when everything hit the fan. It was like I was a stranger to you. Unrecognizable.

Source: Ulises Zind, 41

Day: Friday, April 23
Time: 1:17 p.m.
Location: Saltwater Hall B Mackenzie College Room 216

I'm nervous. Is this part really important? Do I *have* to go to church to "grow" as a Christian? It seems very old school. And why are there so many different services this weekend? Is Saturday-night service when they party with the wine or something after? I don't know what to wear; I don't know how to act. Are they going to baptize me? They better not try to dunk me in water. I'd fight someone. They also better not ask for my money. These are my coins. Yeah ... I'm not so sure about this. I could just text her and tell her I'm sick ... or that I got attacked by a beaver. Those things are looking big in the campus creek.

Source: Kamden Upstin, 18

DAY: SATURDAY, APRIL 24
TIME: 3:01 P.M.
LOCATION: SUDS & STUDS CAR WASH

Father—what am I doing wrong? Tell me. Tell me what it is. I'm willing to fix it all. I don't see it; I don't know where I can improve. In the beginning, it was easier to identify, and fix, my shortcomings. There were times in my life where I was constantly far from you, directly fighting you in others, but that was then, and this is now. I'm with you. My husband and I are with you. I feel like we do everything you ask, but I don't feel any closer to being a mom.

The doctors say be patient. Just be patient. Just be patient. They only want me to continue to be their patient—that's what it is. Ugh. There has to be something I can fix. Something that is keeping me from hearing your voice on this, from seeing the direction you want us to follow.

Help me remove these obstacles from my path, Lord. Help me continue to fight.

Source: Tricia Curtis, 31

DAY: SUNDAY, APRIL 25
TIME: 10:11 A.M.
LOCATION: CRIMSON PARK TRAIL

I can't do it. I can't keep feeling like this on Sundays. I have to tell someone. I can't. I have to. Please give me something else to deal with, God. Anything. I'd rather have problems with addiction than be gay. I'd rather be depressed than be gay.

My family won't look at me. My church will scorn me. What church would let me come through their doors? Is this how I was always supposed to be? I don't even have an empowering "coming out" story. It's just gonna be me crying in the church parking lot and losing all my friends. I want to ask for prayer but I can't. I want to ask for help but I would get hate in return.

Source: Dustin Saudiner, 20

CHAPTER FOUR
The Park

It had to be wasps. One of my greatest nemeses on the planet. But I get it, it's summer and the kids want to use the park, but they're afraid of the wasps. Well, so am I. They could run around at the other parks in the town and let me avoid this battle. That skate park always seems to be a hoppin' spot for the youths. But we want the campus to be a place for people of "all stages and ages" and that means we need a functioning park for some reason. I don't understand some of God's creations. Why make something so vicious? And so buzzy? It's really the buzz. Gives me the shivers to think about it. We had a few close calls last year. I'll give it to them—they are a resilient species. Good thing I have years of training myself. I wasn't sure those summers on my aunt's farm were ever going to be put to use later in my life, but those sunburns and rashes were not for naught. She enjoyed rocking on her porch in the evening with the sun dusting the surrounding fields as I ran around like a chicken with my head cut off from the swarms attempting to protect their own space. They probably didn't understand me either. Why was I throwing rocks and blowing smoke up their homes? I was the big bad monster trying to tear apart everything they had built. They weren't bothering anyone. Except for my auntie. She couldn't let them hurt her beautiful oaks like that. And I was her young warrior to defeat the encroaching parasites. She wasn't "limber" enough to do the dirty work anymore, but she would cook an immaculate meal for me after a long day of battling, so our contract was signed and sealed. Each summer I'd devise new tools to remove the wasps as efficiently as possible. The less risk I undertook, the better. The slingshot was harsh, but effective. The fireworks were a little over the top, and the most likely to cause civilian casualties. The sprays. So many sprays. Impactful in hand-to-hand combat, but the riskiest in the long term. The closer to the hive you had to be the worse the sleep would be that night.

That was then, and this is now. Now, I have money to buy machines. To let all these technological advances in the past decades help me in this battle. Marcus thought I was crazy when I told him I would take it out of my earnings to buy this sprayer, but it's worth every penny. Besides, it's for the kids. I'd rather have them out here enjoying the park than inside picking up bad ideas from God-knows-what they are into these days. If I had any kids, I'd make park time mandatory. Any time outside really. The fresh air is good for you. The sun ain't scary. It builds character to get splinters sometimes. Well, maybe wood chips weren't the best playground material growing up. This rubber or whatever this stuff is doesn't seem as inviting but is certainly safer. When you're a kid you don't always want safer, though. A little danger keeps your senses heightened. Wasps present too much of a threat. Too much of an uncontrollable danger. That's why I'm here. To control the situation.

Day: Monday, April 26
Time: 5:33 p.m.
Location: Curry Skate Park

I think I really connected with him with that email. That was a great idea. He's always on it so it must be his favorite way to communicate. I hope he likes my summer "playlist" of things we should do to make Mom happy. We'll both be in trouble if Mom keeps noticing our bickering. What a mom word ... *bickering*. Whatever. Put some points on my side for trying to be a good stepson. Ugh.

Source: Hauz Metzen, 14

Day: Tuesday, April 27
Time: 11:04 p.m.
Location: Haranna Bedroom

Aye yai yai! What are we going to do about this man? His lack of self-awareness is mind-numbing. His self-centeredness is tiring. And his overall hygiene could only be described as a work in process. And now I'm getting pulled into his mess in the usual fashion. How are his shortcomings somehow laid at my feet? I'm not a part of his problem but Dad thinks it's on me to help be a part of the solution. I have my own problems to deal with. I'm trying to live my life. I'm trying to do me. I don't have time to get this man straight.

That's what needs to happen: Jesus, help my dad see that because he and Mom spoiled their son so much he can't get right at age thirty-seven. Then maybe he'll turn up the parenting a notch so I don't have to. This house would fall apart if it wasn't for me.

Source: Estella Haranna, 39

DAY: WEDNESDAY, APRIL 28
TIME: 5:51 A.M.
LOCATION: UNDISCLOSED FISHING SPOT

Jus' how we like it. Silent. No phones. No pings. No nothin'. Just us. My dinghy. My pole. And the little fishies. Make 'em nice and hungry today, Jesus.

Thank you for these mornings. For these times when I can get away. A lot of people need this, that, and the other nowadays, but you know I've always been simple to please. I'm jus' a fisherman at heart. But good thing that's what you like, huh?

Source: Chapman Herman, 63

DAY: THURSDAY, APRIL 29
TIME: 1:08 A.M.
LOCATION: QUINO BACKYARD

What should I do?

Should I tell them Ronnie reached out to me? No, that will only make it worse. They'll think I'm going behind their backs ... even though that's the only place their son feels safe.

And how do I not betray his trust? I don't think he would be reaching out to his disgraced uncle if he had somewhere else to go. Is this my battle to enter, anyways? Is it on me to help my coward brother fix his son? What happens if I don't? What happens if I do? Who is the one getting hurt in those scenarios? Probably me, as usual.

Give me clarity. Give me wisdom. Give me words that work. Give me words that do something for him.

Source: Wesley Quino, 39

DAY: FRIDAY, APRIL 30
TIME: 8:15 A.M.
LOCATION: HIGHWAY 40

This can't be it. This can't be how I die. In my car? As just another crash fatality? What happened to all the things you had planned for me? Weren't you supposed to take care of me?

Please, God, remove this door. This metal. Get this off of me. This is not how I'm supposed to go. I'm one of the good guys. One of your people. I have so much more to do. No no no no no no no. I don't hear any sirens. Is no one coming to help me? You can't send anyone for me? Get me out of here … I can't breathe, I can't breathe, I can't breathe, I can't breathe … please.

Now … I'm here … in my car … where I spend … this isn't it … I'm sorry … I'm …

Source: Tanner Roughshed, 30

DAY: SUNDAY, MAY 2
TIME: 9:17 A.M.
LOCATION: NEW HAVEN STAGE

Heavenly Father, we come to you in a difficult time today. We tragically lost one of ours this past week and it's never easy for anyone to battle through such an event. As much as we know that you are on the other side, the loss of life will always sting. So we mourn in this time and we ask that you place your hands on the Roughshed family and watch over them and send them as much peace as possible. Guide them through this tragedy. Help them stay close to you through it all.

And let the rest of us in the body be the support beams for their family right now. Open our hearts for them. Help us love on them as best as we can.

We also thank you for the life Tanner was able to live. It was cut too short, but many of us have had the privilege to see him grow into a respectful man and an even better Christian over the past five years. I'm thankful you allowed New Haven to be a part of his life, and for giving him a community to call home.

Death is never easy, but we know you have overcome it and now Tanner gets to enjoy the other side with you.

We pray for your sovereignty in our lives, always.

Amen.

Source: Marcus Garland, 43

DAY: MONDAY, MAY 3
TIME: 7:42 P.M.
LOCATION: FAULKNER BEDROOM

Jesus, why are Mommy and Daddy so sad? Did I do something wrong? Did Salem do something wrong? I bet it was him. He's a good brother, but he breaks things a lot.

I'm excited for the new trips we are going on this summer. I must be a great kid. Mommy said this was going to be the best summer ever. I can't wait.

Thanks for such great parents. And Salem, I guess.

Source: Izzy Faulkner, 6

Day: Tuesday, May 4
Time: 3:16 p.m.
Location: Camden First Bank

Remember when I was going to go broke being a tutor, Dad? Ha! Take that.

But also thank you for the business, Jesus. Thank you for these overeager parents who try to push their dreams on their kids. I'm not saying it's healthy, but me being broke isn't healthy either. Some of these kids need the extra help, but most just need someone to give them more time than their teachers have for them. The school system wasn't great for me so I know how it can leave some kids behind. Luckily, you gave me a dad who wasn't going to let that happen, right? Kidding ... kidding ... you gave me parents I could never thank you enough for.

Source: Angel Zombuka, 28

Day: Wednesday, May 5
Time: 5:53 a.m.
Location: Minterson County Police Station

Let today be a good day, God. Help us be a light in the community. Help us show people that we are there for them. That we care and that we want to listen to them. Help this event go over smoothly and let all parties walk away with a little more patience in their heart, a little more willingness to see things from both sides of the issues. I know we don't always see things the right way, but, really, neither do they. They think they understand the sacrifice we make, but I'm not sure they do. Help me be the right representative for this task. Help me make it mean more.

Source: Danielle Grainger, 33

Day: Thursday, May 6
Time: 1:59 p.m.
Location: Armun Home Office (Closet)

I. Don't. Know. What. Else. To. Do.

Have I not given this part of my life over to you? I'm literally trying to get into the nonprofit industry. A.k.a. make very little money and attempt to make a difference in the long run. Practically a modern-day saint over here. I'm not trying to get into Big Oil or work for Amazon or something, I'm tryna do good! *Let me do good.*

I'm going to start recording these prayers and send them to my parents so they can't tell me I'm not praying enough for you to hear me. I could really do with fewer worry-filled phone calls from them. What I could really *really* go for is some godly intervention in my inbox one of these days with at least a response from a human being. These robots don't feel my kindness seeping through the screen. *Let me seep.*

Source: Yasmine Armun, 24

Day: Friday, May 7
Time: 8:09 p.m.
Location: Silver Stone Business Complex

I can't stop thinking about how he reacted to my good news. Or how he didn't react at all. What was that about? He's never done that. He's always been in tune with me. He's always been my biggest supporter. Was it something I did? Maybe I'm not listening to him right now. God, help me be the best supporter of my husband that I can.

Source: Veronica Chaucer, 36

DAY: SATURDAY, MAY 8
TIME: 10:36 A.M.
LOCATION: CREEKSTONE DRIVING RANGE

Let this obstacle fly away, God. Like these golf balls—let me smash this sickness away from my daughter. She's too young to defeat this by herself. Let me take it on. Give me a swing at it.

Source: Roxy Faulkner, 38

DAY: SUNDAY, MAY 9
TIME: 4:00 P.M.
LOCATION: SUFFOLK PUBLIC LIBRARY

More of this "everything you do is a huge mistake" attitude. That's jus' untrue. I came into the house a little drunk once or twice, and she acted like I was coming home from murdering someone. And she's trying to threaten me with "telling Dad" on me like we are children again? Dad is less sober than ever these days anyway.

I don't understand why she wants life to be more difficult for me. I don't know if I should pray for her life to get better so she stops worrying about mine or if that would make it worse. I pray that you do *something*. Do anything that eases her temples. Give her mind an extended vacation from worrying about me. Should I feel bad that I put my trust in you and don't worry about all the little things like her?

At the end of the day, I'll listen to you before I listen to her.

Source: Leo Haranna, 37

Day: Monday, May 10
Time: 12:16 p.m.
Location: Mrs. Laslo's Class (Rose Mound Middle School Classroom 11A)

Amazingly, remarkably, astonishingly ... through your miracle-inducing powers, we've just about made it through another year, Jesus.

Sure, they definitely looked at their phones just as much as they looked at me. But, to be honest, they can probably learn the same amount on their phone as I can teach at this point. One or two kids acted like they wanted to be here each day, and that's all I can hope for. And this is the third year in a row where I didn't have to restrain myself from kicking one of them in the shin, so that's significant improvement as well.

As always for my end-of-school-year prayer, I pray that over the summer these kids don't forget every single thing I fed them. Help them be safe. Help them stay active (especially you-know-who). Help them grow, physically and mentally, into able-bodied learners who realize how lucky they are to have teachers like me, Patrick, Jamal, Gloria, and the rest of the crew. Except Mrs. Scrant ... she can get lost on her boat in the lake this summer.

Source: Bailey Laslo, 39

Day: Tuesday, May 11
Time: 11:20 a.m.
Location: Merchant Duck Pond

Thank you for all these little beautiful duckies. I always love to see them growing up this time of year. Running around following mama with no clue about the dangers of the world. No clue what's right or wrong. They only know to do as they see. A full little family. I wish I still had my family to run around with. Our family was the best. My dad always oblivious, Mom too tired to correct him, and all us kids making them both go crazy. Seven kids is a lot. Well, eight. I wonder if our little lost baby brother is up there with the rest of them right now. He probably greeted them all. He was always with us. He was here the shortest but had the biggest impact on everyone. He helped us realize that our family would always be the most important thing to all of us.

I pray they are all there with you now, Lord. I pray I get to see them again soon.

Source: Harriett Wallard, 92

Day: Wednesday, May 12
Time: 6:46 p.m.
Location: Sonic Drive-In Stall 14

This can't be how it goes, God. Does everyone else really move on with their life, just like that? Like my best friend didn't just die?

Everyone is praying for me and everyone has me in their thoughts and I still feel alone. I still feel like I let him down. We had so much life left in front of us. Now I can't do any of that without thinking about him. I can't go to Sonic without thinking about his terrible order—ha. I loved him so much.

Everything seems pointless right now. All the messages, all the condolences … help me see that this has a greater meaning. Help me believe that. Help me see how this is supposed to work out for your good in the end. Help me see the point in all of it. Help me see the point in this prayer.

Source: Nick Roughshed, 26

Day: Thursday, May 13
Time: 5:15 a.m.
Location: Crooked Heights Weight Room

Father, thank you for giving me this time with these kids. I know I joke with them—and you—a lot, but I want them to see that someone cares for them. If no one else in their life cares for them, I want them to see that I do. I want them to *feel* that I do. This time is so important in their lives to learn and grow and I pray you help me never take for granted that I have an opportunity to be a part of it.

Please continue to give me the strength, energy, and passion to be someone they can look up to in life. In other words, bless me with the juice!

Source: Oliver Pernell, 47

Day: Friday, May 14
Time: 10:13 a.m.
Location: Morton Bed

Ahh, what's that? A sleepy morning? A lazy morning? Ahh, God, you are too good to me. And on a Friday, huh? Three-day weekend say whaaaa?

Hmm, what's on my list of things to do this weekend? Oh right, I tore that list up last night because I'm an adult and can procrastinate as much as I would like.

Here's to a freaky Friday and a wild weekend. Please help me show up on Monday with all my limbs.

Amen.

Oh, and help out Mrs. Garland. She shouldn't have to stress like that. I've never been to her church, but I know her husband's the pastor. Shouldn't you bless them more? They are cutting it close this year. Look out for them.

Source: Quincy Morton, 32

DAY: SUNDAY, MAY 16
TIME: 2:32 P.M.
LOCATION: JUTTE PUBLIC POOL

God, please, please don't make me save anyone this summer. I've made it the past two summers without having to jump into the pool and I would like to keep it that way. Sure, I can pass the test and I can blow a good whistle, but pulling a whole body out of the water? That doesn't sound like something I'm ready for.

If anything does happen, let it be on someone else's watch. Maybe Brunson? He always acts like he can't wait to save a life. I'm good on all that. I'll take some stubbed toes and dirty bathrooms over touching someone's wet lips. Yuck.

Keep this summer drowning-free and, as always, bless me with a killer tan.

Source: Mario Leflour, 16

DAY: MONDAY, MAY 17
TIME: 4:16 P.M.
LOCATION: KING$ DREAM STUDIO

Is that all I'm worth, 1,225 streams? That's all that these hours mean?

It was not supposed to be like this. It was not supposed to be so ... tiresome. Here I am, struggling for everything, with barely a blip on the radar. Yet, you let these dudes who represent everything wrong in the world pop off and end up on *Late Night* in three months. I've been at it for three years with barely anything to show for it.

A college degree doesn't sound like a bad idea right now.

I pray these streams don't come to define me. Let my skills and my dedication define who I am. Let my voice find value.

Source: Booker Naheem, 21

DAY: TUESDAY, MAY 18
TIME: 10:12 P.M.
LOCATION: POLLIER KITCHEN

I still can't believe what happened to Tanner. He was a good kid. I haven't talked to him in years but we had some good times in high school. He was a bright face. He probably saved us from making some bad decisions a few times too.

Life is short, God. Events like this help everyone remember that, but I hope we never lose sight of it. Help *me* not lose sight of that. Help my prayer life improve and include the people close to me more often. Give me patience to enjoy the little things in life. Help me enjoy these times I still have with my family, my parents, my kids, my friends.

Most of all, I pray for Tanner's family—I know everyone else will move on, but that hurt will stay with them for a long time. The only thing more pressing than that hurt is your love. I pray they feel your love and know it is with them wherever they go.

Source: Cat Pollier, 31

Day: Wednesday, May 19
Time: 11:33 a.m.
Location: Banks Roof

Thanks for another day of work, God. Another opportunity to live my life and another chance to provide for my parents. Please keep my parents safe and healthy. And let this work I'm doing today provide a better tomorrow for all of us. They barely had anything growing up and have done so much just for us to get to where we're at now, and now it's on me to become the provider. Help me carry that weight the best I can.

Also, give some perspective to Mr. Banks's son down there. I see him around mowing yards in the summer and he always looks as miserable as possible. He should be thankful for a dad who's trying to teach him what it means to work and earn money for a living. He's lucky to have parents who can probably afford for him to go to college and get that magical piece of paper. Not everyone is set up for success like that.

Source: Benny Furtan, 22

DAY: THURSDAY, MAY 20
TIME: 8:45 P.M.
LOCATION: 4522 BRIGGUM STREET

How do I keep ending up here, Lord? Where is your strength in me? Aren't you supposed to be with me? That's what I say on the stage. That's what I tell those people in the church. They listen to me and believe my words … but if only they knew. If only they know how broken I was. I would lose everything. That's why I need to defeat this on my own—nobody needs to find out. Nobody needs to know my weaknesses.

Source: Asher Sage, 38

DAY: FRIDAY, MAY 21
TIME: 7:10 A.M.
LOCATION: JOYCE BEDROOM

Father,

Please help this news go over well. I know Zehare is going to fight us on this. I know he will only see the negatives of this summer camp. But I truly believe it is for the best.

Everything I read about it seems to be just the thing he needs. He just needs to go into it with an open heart. Help him see this is only out of love for him. That this is only because we care for him too much to let him move away from you during this time in his life.

Give us the strength to be the parents you want us to be.

Amen.

Source: Helena Joyce, 40

Day: Saturday, May 22
Time: 1:50 p.m.
Location: QuikTrip Pump #5

Help Marcus enjoy our vacation for once. He's always "on." I want him to completely disconnect and be with us. Jonah needs this too. We need a good start to summer. I want them to be free with each other and not constantly compete or keep score. Jonah is at that age … and Marcus has been at that age his entire life. I'd love to avoid double-babysitting duty this week.

Give us this week to enjoy the moments we are all at in our lives. What's menopause anyway?

Source: Emory Garland, 47

Day: Sunday, May 23
Time: 9:32 p.m.
Location: Elling Bedroom

Bad internet? Huh. Guess you don't want me to watch the service today then. I need the extra sleep anyways. But what should the name of our group be? It's exciting that a few people think we are official enough to have a group name. You've guided us toward a few big steps this year, Lord. Amazing Grace Addicts? The AGA? Ehh, that's too churchy. And we preach that we are more than our *previous* addictions, so that wouldn't make sense anyway. I was never the creative type. The Clay Pots? Hmm. Maybe I'll let the group decide.

Source: Chelsea Elling, 58

DAY: MONDAY, MAY 24
TIME: 7:30 A.M.
LOCATION: FAULKNER BEDROOM

Lord, I feel like this is the beginning of a valley for our family. Whatever happens, let us continue to look to you first and believe in the power of your amazing glory. I know the rest of this year will not be easy. It will test me and my wife, it will test my son, and it will probably leave a mark on my daughter for years to come *when* she survives this.

Help me lead my family through this right now. Help me be strong for them. I pray for my daughter's health and I believe in your power to do miracles. Please perform a miracle in her life and heal her, God.

Source: Michael Faulkner, 37

DAY: TUESDAY, MAY 25
TIME: 12:18 P.M.
LOCATION: SAMANTHA'S SOUPS AND SAMMIES EATERY

Father,

How are you doing today? We probably don't ask that enough. I feel it in my own life, that all of my prayers, my thoughts, my conversations with you, well, they're all about me. That's not why I changed my life in there, I changed my life to come out and help other people. To focus on their needs and see how I can help them so they don't make the same mistakes I did. My selfishness is the reason I spent half my life behind bars. Help me live a life focused on others. That's the only way I can see things getting better out here. Every time I focus on me, I feel like I don't belong. That I'm a fake.

I pray for Bones, for Clammy, for Rico, and for the rest of my family still behind bars. I pray they have continued to meet and worship your name in that dark place. I hope they are letting the power of your word guide their choices, not their own desires.

Thank you for this second opportunity you have given me. Do not let me waste it.

Source: Oscar Abbernathy, 61

Day: Wednesday, May 26
Time: 8:18 p.m.
Location: New Haven Youth Room

This feels ... different. I'm not sayin' it's bad. Just different. Do I still belong here? Am I really a "youth" still? Ha. High school is over. Being young and dumb and dependent is over. Now I'm "off to do bigger things" as my parents would put it. I'm thankful that neither of them imploded with stress this past semester. I was worried there for a bit.

I still have this summer, but I can tell everyone is trying to fast-forward to college and jobs and freedom—whatever that looks like. I'm ready for all of that, but also kind of not ready. I'm comfortable. And everything in front of me feels uncomfortable. Help me navigate that. Help me enjoy this last summer with my friends. Help me embrace this moment.

Source: Layla Sacron, 17

DAY: THURSDAY, MAY 27
TIME: 12:08 P.M.
LOCATION: ROSE MOUND MIDDLE SCHOOL CAFETERIA

Our last Chicken Nugget Thursday of the year, Lord. And look what you did for us?

This is amazing ... these aren't chicken nuggets, these are ...

Chicken fingers!

God is good.

All the time.

And all the time ...

God is good!

Ha ha, we sound like our parents; they always say that.

Probably because they can get chicken fingers whenever they want.

True.

We should do a different day next year. Let's switch it up.

Why? What day should we do?

I don't know. Ask God.

Good idea: God, what day should we pray during lunch next year?

Okay. I'm sure he'll answer before next school year.

Agreed. Let's enjoy our chicken while we have it.

Right. Thanks for praying with me this year.

Of course. Want to hang out next week?

Of course.

Source: Bryce Loon, 13, and Louis Dander, 13

DAY: FRIDAY, MAY 28
TIME: 6:16 A.M.
LOCATION: NON-STOP FITNESS ON CHERRY

This is what we've been waiting for since we started on this journey in January. This was going to be the weekend where I proved that I can set a goal and accomplish it. That when I put my mind on something I will not be deterred. That I was coming at 'em different this year, God.

And, well, according to these hips, we did that *ish*! I can't believe the person I'm looking at in the mirror. The way she smiles. The way she holds her head high. The confidence in her eyes. When I look at this woman, that's who I want to be. And, truthfully, we're just getting started. Thank you for believing in me. Thank you for helping me believe in myself.

Source: Bri Verdana, 29

DAY: SATURDAY, MAY 29
TIME: 11:05 P.M.
LOCATION: UPSTIN BEDROOM

Jesus, what should I do? I've been home a few weeks now and my parents keep asking me where I'm going each Sunday. Why am I ashamed to tell them I'm going to church?

We weren't religious growing up, but they didn't hate on Christians. But I can't imagine it not being awkward. I don't want them to think I've changed ... but I have. I think? Isn't that what you want? For us to feel changed. Different through you? That's what the people on campus say. Look at me, I *have* been listening.

Maybe I'll just tell them I've been curing my hangovers at a toxic friend's house. That would be less surprising.

Source: Kamden Upstin, 18

Day: Sunday, May 30
Time: 3:30 p.m.
Location: Lake Walalee

Thank you for this incredible country, Jesus. Thank you for all the servicemen and women who have given the ultimate sacrifice for our country. I know a lot of people like to disrespect them and forget that freedom isn't free, but I'll never forget. I'll never kneel during the anthem. I'll always remember their sacrifice and I'll never forget your sacrifice either. I'm just worried about everyone else. Help these ignorant people who believe everything they see on TV. Help them come to you. I know you'll fix them, and I know you'll fix our country. I'll stand for you forever.

Source: Austin Grant, 57

Day: Tuesday, June 1
Time: 7:25 a.m.
Location: Haranna Bedroom

You know what? This is my summer to not worry about him and his issues. This is my summer to live my best life. Be courted by some handsome summer hunks. I'm writing H.A.G.S. to him in my brain and letting that man-child be. I will not be responsible for whatever state his life is in, no matter what our poor father says.

God, help me focus on my time, my energy, and my future this summer. Help me put the blinders on.

Source: Estella Haranna, 39

DAY: WEDNESDAY, JUNE 2
TIME: 9:34 A.M.
LOCATION: FALDON LAWN

I know each summer I make this prayer and each summer we end up right where we left off last summer, but I know that Jesus juice is real and I know what it can do. Remember that summer camp where you made those kids on the front row faint? That was something else, but I took note of the power. Now, I don't need anything like that, but we've already hashed out that these lawns are the bane of my existence. Every summer I struggle with these blades of grass mocking me, sucking up all my time, removing all joy from my summer. From my perspective, you could either stop all the grass from growing this summer, or give my lawn mower the ability to churn it down at an unheralded pace.

If I were you, giving my mower the juice seems to be the easiest route and the one to cause the littlest uproar amongst the common folk. But I know you like to go big and part seas every now and then, so if the grass didn't move all summer, you wouldn't hear any complaints from me.

So what's it going to be?

Source: Elliott Banks, 15

DAY: THURSDAY, JUNE 3
TIME: 2:58 P.M.
LOCATION: SUDS & STUDS CAR WASH

Another year, another group of students off into the world. That's the worst part about this job: I never know if I did enough. There's no end-of-year meeting where the students sit me down and let me know they were only coming to flirt with the other kids or if they legitimately want to live for you the rest of their lives. That would be nice, but not practical. Half of them are still trying to figure out who they are anyway, let alone who you might be in their life. I can't blame them. I was farther away from you than most of them seem to be, so that's something, I guess. The college years are so important. I wish I could be right there with them, helping them sort through all the pressure and desire for acceptance on campus and lead them down the path you set out for them. I know, that's your job though. I did my part. At least, I hope I did.

Father, please watch over every single one of these kids as they go out into the world and find themselves. It only gets harder from here, but good thing that gives you more opportunities to increase your presence in their lives. Keep all of them safe. Give them all courage to stand up for your name.

Of course, please give a little extra guidance over Layla. She's special and I hope she realizes that.

Source: Wayne Zen, 35

DAY: FRIDAY, JUNE 4
TIME: 1:46 P.M.
LOCATION: JACK COS. BBQ RESTAURANT BACK OFFICE

Please let this be a Goods New Appointment ... we're overdue a GNA.

This is the first one since last year when we decided to be faithful and patient and continue to try on our own. So far, it has not netted any positive results. Don't do it for me, do it for her.

I know we talked last week about taking this summer off from the pressure of starting a family, but I worry that the pressure has become a part of her. I get the sense this isn't something she thinks about once a week but once an hour. I don't want her to get defined by any outcome, good or bad. I want her to be defined by your love.

Source: Graham Curtis, 29

Day: Saturday, June 5
Time: 8:46 a.m.
Location: Goldstern Fridge

No no no no. This cannot be happening. Of course it's happening. This always happens to me. Why did you curse me with such bad luck, God? We both know I can't be late for this. Ahhh. Where are my keys? I could really use some help with this. When do I ask for anything?

Okay, if you won't reveal my keys at least make everyone else late as well. Like an accident on the highway. Well, you know, one where no one gets hurt. Like a bird on the road. Not dead, but alive. Just walking around on the road making everyone slow down and honk at each other and get angry and drive worse, causing more traffic.

Give me a duck, God!

Source: Kristen Goldstern, 46

CHAPTER FIVE
The Breakout Room

I t doesn't need it always, but this room deserves just as much attention as the rest of the place. You could argue it needs extra attention. Extra attention for the place for people who need extra attention. I always hated attention. *Why can't I make the presentation perfect and send it in? Why do I need to present it?* My teachers used to get so flustered with me. Maybe they knew I was going to become a janitor, so they were wasting their time with their statistics and history lessons. I liked my work to do the talking for me. That's why I'm good at my job now. I put in the time in the places other people overlook. The places they think can "wait until next week." Some things can't wait until next week. Some people need to overcome their addiction today. They might not make it to next week, so they come to this room and find peace in my clean tiles and smudge-free windows they look out of and dream of a world where they aren't struggling.

It's funny they call this the breakout room. No one comes in here to take a break. They come here to put more work toward whoever they think they should be. Or whoever their friends and family told them they should be. Or, according to the last service, who God wants them to be. It was good for me to make an appearance at a service. Hadn't been in a while. And it makes me feel like I'm doing recon for my job. I get to sit back, watch, and take note of what areas get the most dirt, the most traffic, the most germy germs. Number-one cause of church absence: sickness. Number-one cause of sickness: germy germs. At least, according to the notes I took from the service. I should try harder to pay attention. It's different when your place of work is a place of worship for everyone else. You could make the argument I spend more time in church than most of the people out there. Not that that makes you a good person. The people who go beyond the auditorium and make it all the way to the breakout room are not always good people either. Recognizing that is the first step, though, so I commend them all. Lots of tears and hard conversations go down in this space. Sometimes people have to visit it more than once. Sometimes people never do. I'm not sure if one is better than the other, but I'm here to make sure it's ready for the first visit or the tenth visit.

The breakout room can also be the only space some people ever visit at New Haven. The self-help-class-only type of people. It's a natural urge. Sometimes you want to fix your problems without involving a higher power. For me, it's an opportunity to advertise my work to the folks who avoid the church at all costs. It's funny to see them wander in during the week like their skin is going to catch flames. Looking for the exit before they make it halfway through the entrance. I can't blame them; most churches are more intimidating than welcoming these days. The random groups and organizations who use this space for their own fun are usually the ones who dirty it up the most too. That's human nature: to leave someone else's sandbox a little dirtier than your own. Good thing this sandbox has me.

Day: Sunday, June 6
Time: 8:11 p.m.
Location: New Haven Breakout Room

That wasn't terrible. I can make it through six weeks of that. I can fake repentance and remorse for six weeks. I've been faking feelings my whole life.

Just help my family give up on me, God. Let me drink myself into a blissful coma. We both know that will end better ... for everyone. The longer I'm sober the more likely I'll do something really terrible. Sober me knows the real me ... and I don't like the real me. It would be better if everyone forgot about me. If everyone moved on with their lives and let me be the drunk that I am. Let me go, God.

Source: Zayn Niro, 44

Day: Monday, June 7
Time: 6:27 p.m.
Location: Jutte Public Pool

Help me enjoy this summer as me, Jesus. This will be the last summer I'm me. By next summer I'll be someone else ... at least in everyone else's eyes.

How do you see me? Who do you want me to be? It doesn't seem right that you would want me to be carrying this weight around my entire life. But do you want me to be cast out of your presence? Away from the community I've come to call home?

Things aren't lining up like they used to. Remember when I used to pray to be taller? Ha. I wish that was still the type of thing I worried about. Life was easier then.

I want life to be easy this summer. I want to be me this summer.

Source: Dustin Saudiner, 20

Day: Tuesday, June 8
Time: 4:45 p.m.
Location: Pre-Tops and Bickles Band Practice (Fermington Garage)

God, please help me not lose my cool on Jugg today. I know it's summer and the temps are rising and so is everyone's attitude … but he's really been testing me lately. I am the unofficial but totally confirmed leader of this band, and he needs to start putting some respect on my musical choices.

I let him wear that stupid helmet when he's banging on the drums, so why does he feel the need to question my every decision? And, of course, Sessy and Margarette don't say anything while they are over there falling in love. I thought we said no intraband relationships. I figured if anyone was going to fall in love it was gonna be me and Sessy. I can handle them, though, but Jugg has got to get it together. If he asks about my mom one more time during practice, I'm going to chuck something at that stupid helmet.

Oh, and please convince my mom to let us open the garage when we practice, I think that would help everyone chill out. Ohh, and please make sure her back surgery goes well too.

Source: Trevor Fermington, 17

Day: Wednesday, June 9
Time: 6:48 p.m.
Location: Norman Porch

I know these past few years have been difficult and I'm not always the first to realize how lucky I am to have my own business, but thank you. Thank you for a business that has supported me and my family for the last fifteen years. For a business that has withstood recessions, pandemics, tornadoes, feral animals (I still can't believe our cameras "glitched" the one night a raccoon pack raided the snack fridge in the back), and me at times. I couldn't have done it without you. I'll always be grateful for the times I've been able to help the people in our community with this "adventure." Really, I've been able to watch my kids grow up in this store, and that's been worth it all. I don't know how much longer we'll last as a pharmacy, or whatever wild idea my wife is anxious to tell me about, but I know I always want to be a store for the "good guys."

Either way, you've done more with it than I ever thought possible. Thank you for that and for whatever may come next.

Source: Rudy Norman, 38

Day: Thursday, June 10
Time: 10:45 a.m.
Location: QuikTrip Pump #6

Breathe ... breathe ... *breathe*. God, let this phone call be the one that turns this into Hot Employment Summer.

No matter what, I know you are good. Breeeeaaathe, Yasmine. Pick up the phone!

Source: Yasmine Armun, 24

Day: Friday, June 11
Time: 2:22 p.m.
Location: Freedom Basketball Courts

This has to be a joke. A "redemption camp"? If I could create a place that would feel like hell on Earth during the summer, that would be it. Do they have no clue about me? About what I want?

I'm not going. I don't care what they take away, what punishment they give me. Those camps are for show. Those kids aren't ever there for you, God. We both know these church kids go there to hook up with each other away from their parents in the summer. I bet if I told them that they would freak out and think I was possessed or something. Everything is so backward. This is bull.

Source: Zehare Joyce, 15

DAY: SATURDAY, JUNE 12
TIME: 7:18 A.M.
LOCATION: TOONEY FARMS

Jesus, thanks for all you have done for me. For the success of my business. For the success of my children. For everything you have given us. We have plenty. More than we could ever ask for.

I always thought we deserved it all. That all the years of hard work I'd put in had justified our wealth. No one gave us a handout and we didn't cut any corners, we put the work in and saw the harvest come in bountifully.

Yet, as I sit here now and look over our land, our possessions, I feel like we missed something. I feel like something is missing in my life. I never treated anyone wrong, though. I got mine and got out of the way. I did what my father taught me and kept my nose out of other people's problems. Is that what you want us to do? Some days I think you're telling me that I should have made others' problems my problems too. That I was supposed to be an active supporter versus a distant observer.

We've given more in the past few years than I ever thought we would, but when is enough, enough? Is it ever enough? What's missing in this empire?

Source: Fallon Tooney, 70

DAY: MONDAY, JUNE 14
TIME: 2:45 P.M.
LOCATION: CURRY SKATE PARK

Hmm. Another year of a church camp that's way too hot and sticky. I want a camp with AC in the dorms, with food that hasn't been sitting in a back room for three weeks, and a place that's real. I'm almost sixteen now, I need a camp that's legit. Not one of these feel-good, formulaic, everyone-comes-to-Christ-at-the-end-of-the-worship-night places. That's not how it works in the real world.

Source: Jonah Garland, 15

DAY: TUESDAY, JUNE 15
TIME: 10:27 A.M.
LOCATION: JUTTE PUBLIC POOL

I pray that boy who cracked his head open yesterday is okay. They said there was a lot of blood ... you know I don't do all that blood. No shot I would have let that happen on my watch—I'm too quick with this whistle. Tracy probably wasn't paying attention. How do you not notice some kids flipping into the pool?

Oh well, an accident at the pool yesterday means today will be completely controlled. Everyone should be on their p's and q's. And I'll be on my perch like an eagle.

Source: Mario Leflour, 16

Day: Wednesday, June 16
Time: 3:21 p.m.
Location: Macary Park Bench

What's the point of all of this? How long do I have to suffer? How low do I have to go?

I'll admit, I'm ready for help. I've been ready for help. I'm ready to do what needs to be done to pull myself up.

Source: Ulises Zind, 41

Day: Thursday, June 17
Time: 11:10 a.m.
Location: Lake Walalee

Jesus, bless you for days off.

Everything is so tense and stressful on the streets. I feel the stress from work seeping into every other area of my life. I see what it does to my relationships and everything else in my life. I don't want to be high strung and distracted with my loved ones, but it's hard to push out something else when that's all I take in at work.

Fill me up with peace and grace so that I can share it with the people around me. Don't let work steal my shine for the rest of my life.

Source: Danielle Grainger, 33

DAY: SATURDAY, JUNE 19
TIME: 7:40 P.M.
LOCATION: LANSING LIVING ROOM

Thank you for another day to spend time with you, Father.

You've given me a long and happy life and I'll always be thankful for that. I feel like I have many years left to live for you so please help me live those to the fullest. Help me always love and listen first.

Please keep all my family in your hands. Don't let them stray from you. Give us the strength to withstand these troubling times and be courageous for you here on Earth.

Continue to watch over Maleek. I haven't heard from him in a few months. Help him feel loved and cared for wherever he is.

Source: Gigi Lansing, 82

DAY: SUNDAY, JUNE 20
TIME: 11:15 A.M.
LOCATION: NEW HAVEN AUDITORIUM

God, this is all too much. I always thought I was strong—I thought our family was strong—but this weight is too heavy. Please lift it for us. Please lift us up and out of this time. Fast-forward us to the times when we are all healthy and happy. When my husband can focus on taking care of his parents. When I can focus on running my business. When my son can enjoy being young and active and free of worries. When my daughter is ... when my daughter can look forward to the rest of her beautiful life because she is going to be able to accomplish anything she wants in this world. Don't let her not even get started on life. That's not fair to her.

Source: Roxy Faulkner, 38

DAY: MONDAY, JUNE 21
TIME: 7:36 A.M.
LOCATION: JUTTE PUBLIC POOL

God, why do they always make us seem so old for these pool aerobics? We are old and frail, but they don't need to speak to us like we are. And just because my internal body clock won't let me sleep in past 6:30 a.m. doesn't mean this is the only time I want to come to the pool and hang out with these other people about to croak. At least my suit is cute. Their suits look like extensions of their skin.

Like I said, I'm about over these "old people" actions ... I'm too hip for all this.

Source: Harriett Wallard, 92

DAY: TUESDAY, JUNE 22
TIME: 8:10 A.M.
LOCATION: JOYCE BEDROOM

Lord, please move in Zehare's heart this week. Humble him. Love him. Open his eyes to how difficult this world can be without you, but how sweet it can be with you by his side.

Source: Helena Joyce, 40

Time: 8:33 a.m.
Location: Highway 62

Straight up, God, let this bus break down right now and I'll hop out the back. I'll be sneaky and go kick it with Fem for a week. His parents don't send him to camps against his will. I cannot spend an entire week up there. I swear I'm going to make it a terrible time for everyone around me.

Source: Zehare Joyce, 15

Day: Wednesday, June 23
Time: 12:55 p.m.
Location: Grace Jenkins Memorial Hospital

Jesus—

Thank you for another day to do this work that changes lives. Thank you for this skill set and this character to give people hope and belief for brighter days. Give me the strength to stay committed to making this hospital a place where people can believe good things can happen and that it's not just a space where sad things take place. I know we can't save everyone, that's your job, but we can still help people live healthier and more fulfilling lives.

Help our staff bring their best to work every day, because it is life or death.

Source: Percy Byrdwood, 50

DAY: THURSDAY, JUNE 24
TIME: 7:55 P.M.
LOCATION: FREEDOM BASKETBALL COURTS

Reps reps reps. That's what I need ... but reps take time and time is money. Each hour that slips by where I'm still a drain on my parents' bank account makes me sick.

They will never say it, but they don't have to, I can see their eyes startin' to fill with doubt. Probably because my posture has been saying the same thing. There has to be some way. Maybe there's a "regular" job out there that would still fill me up the same as these notes?

God, please give me clarity to know what the next step is for me. Give me wisdom to know the difference between my fleshly desires and your plan for me.

Source: Booker Naheem, 21

DAY: FRIDAY, JUNE 25
TIME: 1:16 P.M.
LOCATION: JACK COS. BBQ RESTAURANT

Lord, bless this food and bless this restaurant. Thank you for the serving staff and thank you for summers away from all those wild kids. Ahh, who am I kidding? You know my heart; those kids keep me young. This is right around the time where I get anxious for them.

Are they having a good summer? Are they being transported carefully? Do they need me to pick them up and take them to baseball practice?

You know I know you know I know Bus 49 can be turned into an all-year transportation machine if it needs to be. I'm about transport. Call me Statham.

Anyway, thanks for BBQ in the summer and I pray all my kids are traveling safely.

Amen.

Source: Alfred Santorin, 58

Day: Saturday, June 26
Time: 2:51 p.m.
Location: The Vista Shopping Center

GAWWWWWWD! COME SAVE THESE PEOPLE! THEY WALK AROUND IN THEIR FILTH AND THEY HAVE NO CLUE WHO YOU ARE. SAVE THEM FROM THE ETERNAL FIRE. THIS SUMMER HEAT IS NOTHING COMPARED TO WHAT'S TO COME LATER. THERE WILL BE NO ESCAPE FROM THE WRATH YOU BRING. THE TIME IS COMING SOON! YOUR CHILDREN WILL BE SAVED BUT WHAT OF THE REST OF THESE PEOPLE? HELP THEM REPENT OF THEIR SINISTER WAYS. RELEASE THE GRIP OF THE EVIL ONE FROM THEIR LIFE. MAKE THEM BEND THEIR KNEES AND CALL ON YOUR NAAAAME!

AND THOSE WHO DO NOT BEND TO YOUR GLORY WILL RUE THE DAY! SAVE THESE LOST SHEEP, LORD!

Source: Verl Muncy, 62

DAY: SUNDAY, JUNE 27
TIME: 8:28 A.M.
LOCATION: REDEMPTION SUMMER CAMP

Thank you for this week almost being over. Just as I figured, another typical church camp.

I'm happy you moved in other people's hearts and people came to you, but I haven't felt moved like that in some time.

I'll need to make up some bullet points about the things that stuck with me from this week for Dad. He probably wouldn't like to hear that I learned what happens when you sneak a ghost pepper into someone's food. I'm glad that kid came back okay from the medic.

At least get us home safely and quickly tomorrow, God.

Amen.

Source: Jonah Garland, 16

DAY: MONDAY, JUNE 28
TIME: 10:42 A.M.
LOCATION: HIGHWAY 62

This week was ... different, God. That wasn't what I expected. Those other kids at the camp seemed ... fulfilled. Or something. They just seemed to have less shame about ... you. Do they care less about what others think of them? Maybe they know something more than me.

I wish I would have gone up to the altar when they called. I don't know why I wanted to go up there for real—somethin' told me I should have. Everything seemed a lot more genuine than I thought. Those folks really cared about all of us and they don't even know me. It felt like love there. It felt like my mom.

Next year, I guess.

Source: Zehare Joyce, 15

DAY: TUESDAY, JUNE 29
TIME: 2:15 P.M.
LOCATION: SUNNY BEACH, GALVESTON, TEXAS

This is it, Lord. These are the scenes I never thought I would see again. I'm sure to most of these families this is another regular Tuesday on the beach, but this is life. This is real air. Real salt moving off the thriving current. The sand that washes away only to return to hold strong to its place on Earth.

I lift your name up for letting me be present in this moment. Thank you for giving me the opportunity to visit these places again and to feel your freedom in this beautiful world you have made.

Source: Oscar Abbernathy, 61

DAY: WEDNESDAY, JUNE 30
TIME: 6:54 P.M.
LOCATION: NEW HAVEN YOUTH ROOM

God, please help us have another meaningful night of worship and teaching with you tonight. Help the fire that started in some of these kids' hearts for you over the past week continue throughout this summer and into the school year where they can really start making a difference in their groups.

I know it's easy to proclaim your name and wear the bracelets when you're at a camp with hundreds of other kids doing it, but keep that passion alive and sincere within these kids as they go back to spending time with their peers who are far from you and don't have godly influences in their lives. Help them be unashamed of your name and help them live for you whether it's popular or not.

Amen.

Source: Wayne Zen, 35

DAY: THURSDAY, JULY 1
TIME: 10:48 A.M.
LOCATION: VINTAGE SPIRITS THIRD-FLOOR CUBICLE

Alright alright alright. At least I'm doing better as a dad this summer than Matthew McConaughey did floating through space and time. I give props to you for getting his mom on my side for a few arguments so he at least recognizes I'm not just out here trying to destroy their family. I want to be a part of it—I need to be a part of it. I've invested too much of my life into her, and into him, for this not to work out.

He seemed to really enjoy the water park last week—and I did too actually. My cannonball technique has helped me ease stressful situations more than a few times in life. Maybe that's where I'm going wrong; maybe I need to learn to be a kid with him first before I try to be a dad to him.

Source: Kenny Sturgiss, 37

DAY: FRIDAY, JULY 2
TIME: 5:40 P.M.
LOCATION: ARMUN HOME OFFICE

I can't believe it.

I finally can sign out of work on a Friday again! THANK YOU, JESUS.

I can't describe the weight that has been lifted from me and I can never thank you enough for helping me through the past five months. It got dark there for a little bit but you gave me the light to continue to try, and that's all we ever need for you to do great things.

This company feels like a great fit. My boss seems like a great person. And this paycheck is about to be a great vibe.

Now that I can focus on everything else in my life, help me remember how to be a good daughter, sister, and all the other titles I completely ignored.

Happy weekend, Jesus, and amen.

Source: Yasmine Armun, 24

Day: Saturday, July 3
Time: 8:24 p.m.
Location: Crimson Park Trail

Help Salem get over whatever is bothering him lately, God. I've never seen him so distracted in the few years I've tutored him. I know I've been distracted at times this year too. I hope I'm not rubbing off on him in the wrong way.

I know he's a good kid. I am probably running too short on patience these days anyway. The heat does that to me.

Source: Angel Zombuka, 28

Day: Sunday, July 4
Time: 9:35 a.m.
Location: Garland Home Office

God, on this day we are supposed to celebrate this amazing country you allow us to live in and bask in all of the freedoms you provide us here, I feel less encouraged to celebrate than ever. We are so clouded and confused right now as a country ... and as a church. We don't know what to celebrate, we don't know how to celebrate—everything feels so fickle. We are supposed to cheer for this person and their story one day and then cast them out the next when they don't support our cause. Christians are the most hated group on the internet but the most feared at the polls. I can feel my congregation wanting me to provide the "truth" and tell them exactly what to do, how to act, and how to love, but I don't know if I can do that. I don't know if I always see that truth. And I don't know if you want it to be that simple. Everyone wants the easy answer, and that hardly seems to coincide with your word these days. It's funny, that book is the only good news we can trust sometimes. All I'm certain of is that the Bible was here before me and it will be here after me, and I pray you let me be the best teacher I can be while I'm here with it.

Source: Marcus Garland, 43

DAY: MONDAY, JULY 5
TIME: 12:44 A.M.
LOCATION: SACRON BEDROOM

Only a few more weeks. That's it. That's all I have left in this town with my church family, with my ratchet friends who I can't stand but can't imagine life without, with Fenz. Oh my gosh, I'm not ready for that. How in the world am I supposed to explain to my dog that I'm leaving? If she makes that little whimper sound I'm gonna break down. I can't handle all of this. I wonder if I can take her with me, call her my emotional-support animal—she technically is. She's been there for me the entire time. High school would have been a mess without her. How am I already talking about high school in the past tense? Why is everything moving so fast? Is it too late to change my mind?

Just—just help me go to sleep so I can worry about all of this another time, God.

Source: Layla Sacron, 17

Day: Tuesday, July 6
Time: 3:18 p.m.
Location: Jutte Public Pool

Another one and another one and another one. He was practically telling me to ask how he was *really* doing last night. I wonder how many chances he'll give me to get inside his head before I'm locked out for good. When am I going to pull the trigger? It's just my brother. I changed his diaper. I shouldn't be this afraid of a *talk*. How is this so easy for extroverts? You definitely made life easier for them. It's probably more than that. I'm afraid of losing my extrovert sibling. I need him to tell the waiter my food isn't right. I need him to call the food in. I need him to love himself.

Source: Everett Saudiner, 27

Day: Wednesday, July 7
Time: 12:46 p.m.
Location: Jutte Public Pool

You know what, this has been a great summer so far. And I don't think it's a coincidence that a certain someone has decided to make herself scarce in my daily schedule. I love her and I'll always rock with her, but the house does better when we give each other space. Well, I do better … Dad has been looking a little musty lately. And for some reason my dishes don't get cleaned as often as before. The dishwasher must be broken or something—I'm sure she'll fix it eventually. She can't let things go dirty for too long or she'll blow a pipe. Maybe I'll clean a couple dishes or something. Nah, I'm not gonna lie to you like that.

Now, only if I can game-plan how to keep this scene in check for the entire year, we'll be golden.

Source: Leo Haranna, 37

DAY: THURSDAY, JULY 8
TIME: 9:52 P.M.
LOCATION: FAULKNER BEDROOM

God—
Why is this happening to my sister? Even though I can't stand how much my parents love her more than me sometimes, she doesn't deserve this.

And why aren't my parents telling her? She's smart, she's going to realize something is wrong eventually. We aren't the type of family to take all these vacations "for fun." It's not right that they aren't telling her. These vacations are going to turn into hospital trips around the country soon. Why is this happening to our family?

Please let this happen to someone else.

Source: Salem Faulkner, 15

DAY: FRIDAY, JULY 9
TIME: 10:39 P.M.
LOCATION: CORNER OF TWENTY-THIRD AND LUCK

Okay, it's gonna be okay. This cop is going to be a good cop. All cops aren't bad. All cops aren't racist. It's gonna be okay. You have a reason to be out right now. You have the right to be out right now. You were barely speeding, but if they ask, you are happy to accept the ticket.

This isn't going to turn into a scene. This isn't a movie. This is a regular traffic stop. My life is precious. Their life is precious. Keep this under control, God.

Source: Harrison Barnes, 32

Day: Saturday, July 10
Time: 7:55 a.m.
Location: Green Rivers Bagels & Bites

God, thank you for the answers you've given us the past month. I know they aren't exactly what we wanted to hear, but I feel so much better not being in the dark about what was wrong with us.

I don't want to say or think this, but thank you for not letting it be me. Graham is so much stronger than me, he can accept the fact that he was the one holding us back. He knows my love for him would never falter and that he can still be the man of my dreams. If it was me, I would have crumbled. I've wanted to be a mother before I knew what it meant to be one, and that can still happen. The science is there and the success rate is reasonable. We still have a chance to make a family … maybe not the most traditional way, but we still have a chance. I still have a chance.

Source: Tricia Curtis, 31

Day: Sunday, July 11
Time: 2:20 a.m.
Location: Quino Backyard

I don't like the last exchange, God. The last convo with Ronnie felt like … acceptance. It was like he was at peace with everything. He smiled when I hugged him goodbye. He never smiles.

Should I not give him money? Should I not care for him? I know every "good" thing he has gotten in his life has been conditional … get good grades and you get this. Go to church and you can go there. Be like us and you can be around us. I want to be unconditional for him. I want to be there for him no matter his performance. No matter his appearance. No matter his habits. Love shouldn't be so hard to earn from your parents. Or anyone. If you are always fighting for love you eventually give up. I don't want Ronnie to give up.

Source: Wesley Quino, 39

Day: Monday, July 12
Time: 11:48 p.m.
Location: Upstin Bedroom

It's strange to say, but I'm excited to go back to campus. I'm excited to be around our little group of Christian weirdos who are passionate about you. It's still weird to hear me call myself a Christian. I figured I was gonna go to college and find new drugs to explore, not a religion … but I guess you pop up when we need you the most.

I pray that all of my friends have had a safe summer. That they've been able to spend time with their friends and loved ones back home. I hope they've stayed close to you and continued to read your word—at least more than me. Still room for improvement there. There's just a lot of words I don't know how to comprehend sometimes. It's like it was written in a whole other language first or something.

That's what I need: grow my brain to help me understand more of the Bible.

Amen.

Source: Kamden Upstin, 19

DAY: TUESDAY, JULY 13
TIME: 4:56 P.M.
LOCATION: 4522 BRIGGUM STREET

God, why did you make me love this stuff? I hate this shit. But I love this shit. I hate this shit. But I need this shit.

You don't want me to get better. That has to be it. If you cared I would have already been caught and someone would already be helping me. Ahh, who would help me? There is no me in the Bible. Just children's stories about fish and bread. I'm not a child anymore; those stories don't apply to me. I'm a man who can't face his fears. What kind of man is that? I am no man. I am this shit. I am no man. I am this shit.

Source: Asher Sage, 38

DAY: WEDNESDAY, JULY 14
TIME: 1:33 P.M.
LOCATION: SEWARD LAWN

Good God Almighty, would you look at the size of that trunk?

These roots are my mortal enemy. Every year I send up a prayer that you would pull these trees out of the Sewards' yard with a magical windstorm, and every year I'm sitting here under the sweltering sun wondering why my prayers go unanswered.

Tuhhhhhh. It's not worth my time to work around these wooden snakes on the ground. They want to ruin the means of my business and my livelihood. Would you let them ruin my business like that? Maybe that's what I should secretly let happen ... but then my real livelihood would be at stake if Boss Banks found out what I did to his mower.

You remember that summer when I accidentally ran over a *few* rocks and Boss Banks saw what it did to the blades, so he decided to toss pebbles in my direction throughout the summer to see how I liked it? That's the type of retribution I'm looking at.

Anyway, I'm still waiting for that summer miracle of dead grass to happen. Any day now ...

Source: Elliott Banks, 15

DAY: THURSDAY, JULY 15
TIME: 6:09 A.M.
LOCATION: TOONEY FARMS

I know what you want me to do, Father, but I don't know if I can do that.

Our land has always been the pride of our family. Each generation has tended to it as carefully as we would our own children, and then grew it and multiplied it as such as well. You know what my grandfather would say: "A man with no land is hardly a man." I know he wouldn't approve of this calling you've put on my heart. My children will probably fight me on it. My siblings will try to stop me if they can.

All these little "coincidences" you brought about in the past couple years—I know you were slowly putting together the puzzle pieces for me. I was never very good at those. She would have seen the picture a long time ago. She was always better about seeing the bigger picture than me. She would love this crazy idea of mine. That's how I know it's meant to be.

Give me the courage to make the right decisions with the right people in mind, Father.

Amen.

Source: Fallon Tooney, 70

CHAPTER SIX
The Kitchen

When I was young, they didn't have kitchens in churches like they do now. My dad would shake his head in disbelief at the kitchen operations some churches have within their walls. Ours is still modest, which means fewer faucets for me to clean, so I'm not complaining. Sinks are a petri dish for bacteria. And trash cans. And fridges. Most things in the kitchen, I guess. But when the bread breaks, the faith is made. Or some cheesy church saying like that. Community is centered around the food table, that much is true. We all know that. Churches know that. The more food floating around a building the more energy and activity will follow. That's simple physics. The result of that? A busy kitchen. Probably the second-busiest room in the entire building.

Food has always been one of the best ways to communicate your feelings to others. Don't know how to put a ring on it? Throw it in the champagne. Can't get through the breakup conversation? Buy a "Just Friends" cookie cake. Want to remove someone from your life for good? Order them the crab cakes. Well, if they're allergic to crabs, of course. I can't believe she took that so hard … it was an honest mistake. A meal can say more than a conversation ever could. Or, at a minimum, it can be the setting for the conversations in our lives. That's why kitchens are so important: it's where we prepare to communicate with those in our lives. Even better, it's where we talk to our bodies. To ourselves. The food you eat is how you communicate to your body what you think about it. I hope everyone is kind to their body; there is enough hate and dismissal from everyone else. The kitchen is where transformations start. Where change is catalyzed. I do enjoy seeing the body transformations people go through and post on Facebook. I saw that one girl who goes here shared her pictures—good for her. That's the inspiring content I support. It almost inspires me to start posting my own before-and-after pictures of my transformations—not of this hardened body, but my cleaning jobs. It seems silly, but I think that's what people like on the social medias. I'm too humble for such a spotlight on my work. I'll keep the photos on my phone private for now, but if I ever need to become an "influencer" for some extra cash, I'll always have that backup plan. Ha. Wouldn't that be funny? Me posting photos of cleanings for people to see. The youth pastor would probably love it, he's always talking about something on social media during the updates. Zen? Wen? Something like that. Seems like he's connected with his flock. Maybe I should ask him to send out a post to the kids in the church to stop leaving food out in this kitchen. Unless they want the ants to boost up the attendance numbers. I'm not looking forward to that clean.

DAY: FRIDAY, JULY 16
TIME: 12:42 P.M.
LOCATION: HOMELAND MANUFACTURING LUNCHROOM

I'm going to miss these lunch breaks, God. I'm going to miss my chair and my table and my lunch box and the creaky window that always lets the breeze in. I'm going to miss this place.

I can't believe it's been thirty-two years with this company. I've seen many people come and go, but I always felt you wanted me right here. Impacting everyone's lives in my special way. I hope I did what you wanted me to. I hope I leave this workplace better than I found it.

Source: Rangar Ramezus, 64

DAY: SATURDAY, JULY 17
TIME: 6:40 P.M.
LOCATION: SWEETIE'S TAVERN PARKING LOT

Is this what those meetings are supposed to do to you? They make you feel like you are letting everyone in there down just by showing up at the watering well. This is my place, God. This is where we have had many fights in the rain—me yelling at you as I stumble to my car and you looking down on me in disappointment, I'm sure. That's us, just a couple always bickering at each other. We are at the end of our line though, huh?

Okay, let's agree to disagree on me going cold turkey. How about moderation? I can do a few in Sweetie's and be okay. I used to do that all the time back when I had people to drink with.

Source: Zayn Niro, 44

DAY: SUNDAY, JULY 18
TIME: 6:13 A.M.
LOCATION: GARLAND HOME OFFICE

What would it be like to sleep in on a Sunday? Asking for a friend.

Source: Emory Garland, 47

DAY: MONDAY, JULY 19
TIME: 2:27 P.M.
LOCATION: CURRY SKATE PARK

An intervention? For me? I've never been so sick in my life! I am the band—what are they thinking? Where will they practice? My head is still spinning from that "lunch." And they did it at my favorite spot. The disrespect is craaaaazy. And Jugg's smug face sitting there all quiet the whole time ... I know he was the mastermind behind it. He's lucky I had a full plate of tots in front of me or I would have smacked that smug right off of him.

God, am I in the wrong here? Or did I just get stabbed in the back by my so-called best friends and you are already plotting justice for me? If I may suggest some Old Testament justice, I think that would be appropriate. A plague on all their future band practices without me would be wonderful.

They're done to me. On to my next band that will be much better.

Source: Trevor Fermington, 17

DAY: TUESDAY, JULY 20
TIME: 10:36 P.M.
LOCATION: JOYCE BEDROOM

Lord—

Thank you thank you thank you for the small steps you have moved Zehare to take since the camp. I know a life for you isn't developed over a week, but we all start somewhere, and we are all at a place far from you when you find us. It fills my heart to see him being the kid I know he can be and, hopefully, turn into the young man who lives for you. I know this is the best time for us to get him turned to you before he leaves our house and goes out into the world.

Please help us be parents who turn him toward you and away from us. Please watch out for my baby boy when I can't.

Source: Helena Joyce, 40

DAY: WEDNESDAY, JULY 21
TIME: 8:18 P.M.
LOCATION: SAUDINER BACKYARD

That was terrifying. I don't know how much longer I can keep hiding these feelings. This is all becoming a slippery slope and causing me to do things I've never had to do before.

I've never had to lie to my parents before ... now half of what I do is under cover. Looking into my dad's eyes and lying to him about where I am or who I'm with each weekend is crushing me on the inside.

I know this is the opposite of what you want, but you are supposed to be the planner of my life. I'm supposed to follow the path you set before me, but this path has never been foggier.

Source: Dustin Saudiner, 20

DAY: THURSDAY, JULY 22
TIME: 7:16 P.M.
LOCATION: NON-STOP FITNESS ON CHERRY

This feeling is different. This feeling of being noticed is ... intoxicating. I see why hot people always act like they can do whatever because they're drunk off their pride. It has been nice at times, I'm not gonna lie. But I didn't do all of this for other people's appreciation, I did this so I can appreciate myself. Lord, help me continue to change my life for the better. Help me focus on working toward my own standards. Help me minimize the opinions of others in my life, good or bad. This body is a temple and it's going to be one that stands for something.

Source: Bri Verdana, 30

DAY: SATURDAY, JULY 24
TIME: 9:35 A.M.
LOCATION: CHAUCER BEDROOM

This is the hard part ... when I don't feel like I have the answers, knowledge, or relationship with you to lead people in the right direction. I hope I was encouraging to Michael the other day. I can't imagine what he is going through with Izzy and his family right now. That's something I've never had to deal with, and I can't thank you enough for that.

But this is part of being a leader for the men in this group. I want them to come to me when they don't know where else to go. That's why I started this Bible study and why I need it too. We all need someone to lean on here on Earth while you're handling everything else around us.

Jesus, I lift up Michael, Izzy, and the entire Faulkner family right now, and I pray that you watch over them and hold them tight in your hands. I pray for Izzy's health and that you heal her so she can go back to being the beautiful light that you created her to be.

Source: Keith Chaucer, 34

DAY: SUNDAY, JULY 25
TIME: 11:15 A.M.
LOCATION: NEW HAVEN PARKING LOT

As always, Lord, please help us watch over this church while they continue to develop disciples and create a Christ-centered community for the rest of the town.

Help us keep this traffic under control, and help keep that homeless man away this time. If he comes up again I'm letting Mendez take that one; he smelled disgusting last time.

Thank you for these Sunday mornings where I can play my part in your kingdom.

Amen.

Source: Danielle Grainger, 33

DAY: MONDAY, JULY 26
TIME: 7:35 A.M.
LOCATION: CREEKSTONE GOLF COURSE TEE 1

Jesus—
Don't let these golf lessons go to waste. I haven't been crafting this swing all summer to come up short now.

Let the fairways be smooth and the traps be small.

Source: Percy Byrdwood, 50

DAY: TUESDAY, JULY 27
TIME: 10:44 P.M.
LOCATION: METZEN MAN CAVE

Dear God, thank you for a very … easy summer. Spending time with Kenny—I'm still not going to call him "Dad"—helped us take steps forward. He is still the cheesiest person on planet Earth, but that's better than being flat-out frustrating.

He just needs to understand that my mom was already hard on me to be the perfect son, which, last I checked, I'm not far off, so he never needed to come in and be the second iron fist. I don't need two enforcers; I can live with my mom and my friend though.

Thank you for working on this friendship and giving me someone to talk to that isn't going to "parent" me about every topic. I need that.

Source: Hauz Metzen, 15

DAY: WEDNESDAY, JULY 28
TIME: 12:55 P.M.
LOCATION: HILTON HEAD ISLAND BEACH

So this is what vacation feels like? I could get used to this … for a while. I've been working so much the past two decades that I barely know how to slow down anymore. Or what it even means to slow down.

My kids were right, though, I need this time away. I'm still thinking about my other kid though—my business baby. I've never been away from her for this long. I wonder if people can tell I'm not in the store. I'm still unsure what pivot makes the most sense, but I feel like a change is the best path forward.

Lord, give me clarity on this next step in my life. Help me follow the path you've laid out before me and live the way you call me to.

For the first time in a minute, I don't have the answers, but I know you do. So please help me find peace in that.

Source: Rudy Norman, 38

DAY: THURSDAY, JULY 29
TIME: 10:44 A.M.
LOCATION: MERCHANT DUCK POND

A lot has changed in this world since Momma squeezed me out all those years ago. She was a real warrior. She was an expert by the time she had me. There was no way I could have had as many as she did. Hell, I was over it after one. One was all I needed—and all I could take. She was such a fireball, just like her grandma that way. I knew she was different when she made that girl her "girlfriend" in third grade. I should have paid closer attention to her little quirks, but I thought it was a phase.

All the names she got called growing up—outside and inside the church—I can't blame her for running away from you. I wish she knew she didn't have to run away from me too. My love for her never dulled, and you know that. Through all the fights, tears, and the sickness that took her away from me, my love never changed. A mother should never bury her child. That wasn't fair for you to put that on me.

I pray she knew how much I loved her.

Source: Harriett Wallard, 92

Day: Friday, July 30
Time: 7:33 p.m.
Location: New Haven Parking Lot

A "summer splash"? Really? Water games and laughter? What a joke. This church is really desperate for these folks' money. God, if you are there, help these fools wake up and see the schemes this place is putting on them.

Source: Theresa Franklin, 16

Day: Sunday, August 1
Time: 10:25 a.m.
Location: Silent Night Coffee Shop

I don't know why I ever thought I could fix him, why I thought I could turn him toward you. I thought I was stronger than he was. I see now that this was never going to work between us. I truly loved him, and he only seemed to love more of himself over the years. Now, this is the only place where I can spend time with you safely. He doesn't want me to take our child to church because he thinks I'm brainwashing her to be afraid of him. If only he could see that his actions are what is terrifying our baby girl. For her sake, I can't let him be around her much longer. Please, help me escape this mess I made. I need your help, Lord.

Source: Beiba Palmandi, 45

DAY: MONDAY, AUGUST 2
TIME: 8:37 P.M.
LOCATION: TARGET AISLE 17

This can't be right—a stock boy? Is this really what's in store for me in my life? Stocking these aisles with canned fruits and beans is decidedly not it. There was no square for this on my vision board, Jesus.

I guess this will just be the low point that I laugh about when I make it to the top. That place seems farther and farther away right now.

Jesus, help me believe that distance is achievable. Fill me up with faith to see this as only a moment in time that will help me get to the next moment.

Source: Booker Naheem, 21

DAY: TUESDAY, AUGUST 3
TIME: 3:05 P.M.
LOCATION: GARLAND LAWN

Are you playing a joke on me? Is this how you're getting back at me for all those lawns with missed edges? By putting the sun right on my shoulder the day I'm doing the pastor's lawn? What kind of twisted fate is this?

This is the only lawn Boss Banks will check on today, so it *must* be perfect. He legitimately brought out a ruler two summers ago and apologized to the pastor because I was off by centimeters. The worst part was the pastor's son sitting inside in the cool AC watching me get embarrassed. I shouldn't even be here really. His son should be out here putting in work. If he pulls up and walks right past me and into his house with a frozen lemonade like he did last summer, I might have to teach my man a lesson in hospitality.

Heavenly Father, I know I can complain a lot and ask for crazy miracles sometimes, but this is serious. I need you to black out the sun today so I can craft this lawn like never before. I need the sweat from my brow removed and the thirst in the back of my throat quenched from that eternal well. Let me mow this lawn like your son would.

Source: Elliott Banks, 15

DAY: WEDNESDAY, AUGUST 4
TIME: 6:35 A.M.
LOCATION: WAFFLE HOUSE

It's August, Lord, you know what that means: time for me to make sure my skills are as fresh as necessary to be the ultimate transporter for all my children.

I know you know I know you know I'm not as sharp as I used to be. I can't make all the turns with ease like I used to. My "mean" voice doesn't carry as much fear in it for the kids like it did back in the day. They watch too many of those creepy movies to be afraid of me anymore. It was always a loving fear anyway. But I have a few tricks up my sleeve this year to make sure the respect I deserve is still coming my way.

"Look at me ... I am the captain now."

Oh yeah, that's good.

Father, help me have a safe year on the roads and watch over these kids as they continue to learn and grow in this crazy world.

Source: Alfred Santorin, 58

DAY: THURSDAY, AUGUST 5
TIME: 11:45 A.M.
LOCATION: GRACE JENKINS CHILDREN'S HOSPITAL

Jesus, thank you for all the new friends I'm making at the hospital!

These kids are all so different, but at least we always have time to play together. I'm going to have lots of time to play with no school this year.

Please help Mommy and Daddy with whatever is wrong with them. I know something is wrong because they always whisper about bad things and that's all they ever do anymore.

Thanks for making Salem so nice lately too. He has never been this nice to me before. It's weird ... but I like it.

Amen.

Source: Izzy Faulkner, 6

DAY: FRIDAY, AUGUST 6
TIME: 7:28 P.M.
LOCATION: MORTON GARAGE

Another glorious weekend to erase my brain from all the nonsense we went through this week.

God, if you could kindly remove all future "IT overhauls" from my life that would be much appreciated.

Let this weekend be one with no mention of the words *software*, *installing*, or *data protection*. Maybe I should go to church. Mrs. Garland would be surprised to see me away from my window, I'm sure. That would be a nice change of pace from our usual stress-inducing convos. I thought she was about to start tearing up last time she came through.

Eh, maybe I'll go next week. Still waiting for you to do something good for them.

Source: Quincy Morton, 32

DAY: SATURDAY, AUGUST 7
TIME: 2:16 P.M.
LOCATION: BRANSON AND FIFTY-SEVENTH STREET

I'm tired of being exhausted; and exhausted from always being tired. It's not even the lack of food or water or anything real right now. I'm tired of all the looks. The eyes of these people who don't know me making assumptions about my life. About what I did to be in this position. They wouldn't believe who I used to be. How successful I was back when you still looked out for me. They won't even give me a bottle of water. I'm not worth a bottle of water. I wish this was all a dream. I wish I could wake up next to my wife and hear my kids crashing through the door demanding breakfast. I'd smile knowing we had all the breakfast we needed downstairs. Just steps away. Honestly, we had way more than we needed. We had plenty to give, but we never went out of our way to help those who look like me now. I never thought twice about the person on the corner. And now I'm the person on the corner. Where is your redemption in that, God?

Source: Ulises Zind, 41

DAY: SUNDAY, AUGUST 8
TIME: 5:38 A.M.
LOCATION: ABBERNATHY BEDROOM

Lord, please calm my nerves today. I knew this was going to happen. I knew I was gonna get all excited over nothin'. It's not like I didn't live in that place for twenty years of my life. Life is funny … those first few years all I did was daydream about killing myself so I didn't have to wake up to one more morning behind those bars, and now I'm anxious to get back. This time as a visitor and hopefully as someone who can connect with those human beings on a level they understand. That's what I want them to see—that they are human beings who deserve a second chance, who deserve your love.

I'm starting to see how this was your plan all along. This has to be why I'm here. To live in this moment to spread your message to those who need it most.

Speak through me today and help me cherish these moments where I can provide light to a darkness I know all too well.

Source: Oscar Abbernathy, 61

DAY: MONDAY, AUGUST 9
TIME: 4:30 P.M.
LOCATION: CROOKED HEIGHTS PRACTICE FIELD

You smell that, God?

Smells like August. Like smelly locker rooms and athletes with bruised shins and stepped-on toes. Smells like voluntary conditioning. Smells like the film room after sessions that make young men cry followed by sessions that fill them with pride. Smells like hearts beating and weights clinking. Smells like competition that makes everyone better, for benchwarmers to become starters and for starters to become Friday-night heroes. Smells like huddles and puddles of sweat, like coaches shouting out scary threats. Smells like ball. Smells like me.

Never take this smell away.

Source: Oliver Pernell, 47

DAY: TUESDAY, AUGUST 10
TIME: 9:10 P.M.
LOCATION: CLAREMORE BUS STATION

God,

Why did you put me in this position? I hate this feeling—this coat of guilt I can't remove. What am I supposed to do? It's either feel like this or have a hungry child at home. I'd rather steal this money than see my child cry himself to sleep at night from hunger. These people have plenty—more than they need—and I can't afford to take care of my child. How is this world so unfair?

If I'm going to sin at least it's for a good cause. I don't see any other way to save him. I thought you cared for the widows and the children and the poor. We are all three, and things continue to get worse.

Source: Toni Gentle, 39

DAY: FRIDAY, AUGUST 13
TIME: 10:25 P.M.
LOCATION: CURTIS HOME OFFICE

I can't shake this cloud of disappointment surrounding me. I didn't think I was going to feel this way. The worst part is I can't talk to her about it. I saw the relief in her face when they said I was the issue. That was bittersweet. I didn't want it to be her ... but until now, it didn't hit me that I could be the one to blame.

Then the next day she hits me with an entire report of our "next steps." Can I get some time to take this in? She's already making appointments and phone calls and I can't keep up with it all.

I thought I was stronger than this is what it comes down to.

Source: Graham Curtis, 30

DAY: SATURDAY, AUGUST 14
TIME: 6:16 A.M.
LOCATION: UNDISCLOSED FISHING SPOT

Did you see that robot shootin' that basketball on the computer? This world is changing so fast. No one likes to make time for things that can't be done instantly anymore. I've always been a slow-cooker type of guy, myself. You know that though ... you know me.

My honey gets caught up in all that flashiness sometimes. She wants to be seen as young still, I can see that. I like being old and slow. It takes time to look this good.

Thank you for getting us to this point in life. I hope we never change.

Source: Chapman Herman, 63

DAY: SUNDAY, AUGUST 15
TIME: 10:40 P.M.
LOCATION: FAULKNER BATHROOM

Word must be out in the church. People are talking about us. All these people I've never talked to before coming up and asking me how I'm "holding up"? Why do they care? We've never talked before. Except maybe if you yelled at me to stop running through the parking lot. I don't like all of this attention. Izzy likes the attention. She's the talk of the church, just like she always liked. I don't think she understands why she's getting all the extra love, or maybe she doesn't want to understand.

I have a feeling school isn't going to be the same this year. Everyone talks in this town. I hope my teachers don't say anything or ask me anything. Only why my homework is late. I just want normal conversations for a break. I want things to be normal again.

Source: Salem Faulkner, 15

DAY: MONDAY, AUGUST 16
TIME: 10:31 A.M.
LOCATION: MERCHANT DUCK POND

God ... I'm scared for Juniper. I'm sorry I left the back gate open—I'm dumb for that—but please bring Juniper back. She isn't a street dog anymore. She needs to be inside with us. And there is a storm coming tonight ... this is terrible. I'm such an idiot.

Please, please, please keep Juniper safe. Help her find her way home. Bring her back to us.

Source: Miles Branch, 10

Day: Tuesday, August 17
Time: 3:20 p.m.
Location: Jutte Public Pool Bathroom

Why did you let that happen, Jesus?

That was extremely embarrassing. I'm the lifeguard. I'm supposed to save people, not be saved.

Did I really look like I couldn't swim?

This is bad … this is very bad. They're gonna make me retake the test and I'm gonna get let go and then I'm gonna need another job and then I'm gonna have to go back to working at the snow-cone stand and then I'm gonna be sticky every day again and then I'm gonna get swarmed by bees again … uh-uh, I'm not going back. I'm not being a sticky human anymore. I grew out of that. Maybe this was the wake-up call I needed. I know I can swim—I'm a freaking fish! I need a confidence boost, that's it. I can do this. I can be a guardian of life.

Source: Mario Leflour, 16

Day: Wednesday, August 18
Time: 5:25 p.m.
Location: Homeland Manufacturing Packing Room

The girls in the office are so sweet here. They make me feel so old but that ninety-day cake was delicious.

I'm impressed they have that many pictures to keep the countdown going. I've never been one to want to be in front of the camera. I'd rather make sure everyone is smiling and enjoying themself. Each picture they send brings back a flood of memories—most that I've forgotten, of course—but each one makes me smile. I never stopped to realize how much work and the people in it have been a part of my life. I'm so grateful you led me here and let me grow up here. I didn't know anything about anything when I started, and now I at least know a little about everything. Not a lot, but enough to be dangerous!

Who are these people going to make fun of for being the old person in the room when I leave?

Source: Rangar Ramezus, 64

DAY: THURSDAY, AUGUST 19
TIME: 1:57 P.M.
LOCATION: GRACE JENKINS MEMORIAL HOSPITAL

We can't afford this. This is all wrong, God. I'm never gonna hear the end of it from my mom. She never wanted me working on-site anyways. She's gonna say something about our family curse, but it was just an accident. Accidents happen on-site. I've broken worse. I'll be back up on my feet, or reconstructed feet, in no time.

But I know we can't afford for me to stay here. I need to get out of here as fast as possible.

All I have is the money I've been saving to move out. If we use that at least we won't be in too much debt, but then everything I've been working for is gone. Just like that.

Where did that stupid dog come from anyway? That person should be paying for all this, not my family. Not us. Not me.

Source: Benny Furtan, 22

DAY: FRIDAY, AUGUST 20
TIME: 8:45 P.M.
LOCATION: NON-STOP FITNESS ON CHERRY

That's it. He needs to move out. The nerve of that *mmmmh* ... to leave a note to me about "someone needing to clean the kitchen" is a complete joke. Like all of Mom's duties haven't fallen on me since she died. But if I bring up sharing any of her work a "split is the only thing that makes sense." He just likes his split as small as possible. There is no reasoning with him. The only way for him to grow up is for all his crutches to be removed. Dad is practically removing himself naturally anyway and now it's my turn. I can't lift one more finger in the name of Leo Arvizu Haranna.

I would ask for you to help him mature but I'm not sure he's worth that miracle.

Amen.

Source: Estella Haranna, 39

DAY: SUNDAY, AUGUST 22
TIME: 2:00 A.M.
LOCATION: NIRO BASEMENT

When did I become unwelcome everywhere? I used to be the guy everyone wanted at the party. I used to be that person who got the party going. Then everyone else decided I crossed the line, and I had no say in my life anymore. Everyone else's opinions mattered more than my facts.

I used to hate it—I still hate it—when they ask, "How did a Christian let himself go?" Like we aren't the ones who need you the most. That's the difference between a Christian and someone who is *spiritual*. We realize how broken we are and how much we need you in our lives as a Savior and Lord. Not a journal to talk about our feelings. Not a candle to create an essence. Not some stones to wear around our necks. We need you to be everything we can't be in this world.

I don't like to be aware of how broken I am at times. But at least I know I'm broken.

Source: Zayn Niro, 44

DAY: MONDAY, AUGUST 23
TIME: 10:10 P.M.
LOCATION: TOONEY FARMS

Lord, thank you for putting Cynthia on my side. I know I need her support to make any of this happen.

I can tell the board is hesitant to hear me out, but they've trusted me with all the decisions in the past that have amassed us this wealth—and the responsibility that comes with it. I pray they see this responsibility is too large for any one person to carry. Many people need to take ownership of what we have built. I believe the more voices we have represented in these conversations around the future of our land the better the outcome for this community. This community helped raise me and now I'm blessed to be in this position to ensure its longevity and ability to raise future generations of men and women who choose love.

That's what I want this land to represent: I want it to be a city on a hill for you.

Let your will be done here, Lord.

Source: Fallon Tooney, 70

DAY: TUESDAY, AUGUST 24
TIME: 4:22 P.M.
LOCATION: WACHOWSKI LIVING ROOM

I've never seen anything so beautiful.

God—above all else, watch over this child. Let this beautiful girl be blessed with your protection every day of her life. Help her achieve anything she wants. Help her grow into all that she can.

Help me be the best dad I can. My entire life is for this little girl now. Don't let me get distracted with anything else. Give me the strength to guide her through this dark world.

Source: Erik Wachowski, 37

DAY: WEDNESDAY, AUGUST 25
TIME: 7:38 A.M.
LOCATION: GRANT BEDROOM

You see? You see what they are doing to our schools? This fake history they are trying to rewrite in our books? You can't just remove people like me, like my dad, and like my grandfather who helped build this country from the ground up. This is horseshit ... excuse my language. But this has got to stop! Just because you are too soft to take the truth of your place in history doesn't mean you can change it. I understand not everything was perfect, but life isn't perfect and neither are people. That doesn't mean you can "cancel" their lives.

Save our schools from all this softness. Save my grandkids from this era of entitlement.

Source: Austin Grant, 58

DAY: THURSDAY, AUGUST 26
TIME: 12:40 P.M.
LOCATION: ROSE MOUND MIDDLE SCHOOL CAFETERIA

I thought we were choosing a new day this year?

Well, you're the one who sat down next to me like we were gonna keep praying over our lunches or something.

What? You're too cool to pray over lunch now?

No. But I am fourteen now and that feels a little old to be praying with my friend in the cafeteria.

You're barely older than me. It's not that big of a difference.

You wouldn't understand. You're still thirteen.

Whatever. So we just gonna pray in silence then?

Yeah, like adults do.

Seems weird ....

Trust me. That's how we are supposed to do it.

Fine. But heads up, I'm going to pray that you stop acting like you know more than me now.

And I'll pray that you grow up quick.

I'll take it.

Source: Bryce Loon, 13, and Louis Dander, 14

DAY: FRIDAY, AUGUST 27
TIME: 6:32 P.M.
LOCATION: FERMINGTON GARAGE

Okay, okay, okay, maybe I was a bit in the wrong. I see that now. I'm not that prideful to think all of my decisions were the correct ones—just most of them.

But, luckily, I'm not above forgiveness ... and I hear their new "band leader" faked his credentials. Dude can't even memorize lyrics—what a simp.

Please let this meeting go well. Please let this summer just be a laughing sidenote ten years from now while we are filming our world-tour documentary.

I miss the band. I miss my friends.

Source: Trevor Fermington, 17

Day: Saturday, August 28
Time: 5:12 p.m.
Location: Lansing Living Room

This year is flying by, Lord, as they all do now. And still, I haven't heard from Maleek. I don't know why he is so stubborn, like the rest of that side of the family.

Open his eyes to see that people care for him. Open his ears and let him hear my prayers for him. Open his heart to you and those who only want the best for him in his life.

He's been through so much. I know he doesn't want to let people in his life anymore, but that's what he needs. I'm what he needs. You are what he needs.

Bless Maleek and bring him home.

Amen.

Source: Gigi Lansing, 82

DAY: SUNDAY, AUGUST 29
TIME: 2:25 P.M.
LOCATION: CRIMSON PARK TRAIL

Finally twenty-one. Now I can finally drink these thoughts away—in front of people, at least. Cover up my true self in the name of a good time.

But what if I do something gay while I'm drunk? What if I start flirting with the wrong people? I don't even *do* gay stuff, I just … I don't know.

Do you want me to change, God? Or do you want me to be who I really am and still be one of your children? I'll be the black sheep of your family then ….

Source: Dustin Saudiner, 21

DAY: MONDAY, AUGUST 30
TIME: 6:45 A.M.
LOCATION: QUAKER COMMON CEMETERY

I'm still waiting, God, I'm still waiting on the bigger picture. Still waiting on when I will stop expecting him to text me about the game last night. Still waiting for someone to tell me this is all a joke. Still waiting for my life to get pieced back together. But even if that happened, I would still be missing a piece—his piece.

Will I feel like this for the rest of my life? Will this fog ever lift? Half of me doesn't want it to, because that means I'll be like everyone else—moving on with their life like nothing happened.

It's becoming harder and harder to see your goodness in this world, God. I'm scared I'm losing the ability to find it.

Source: Nick Roughshed, 26

CHAPTER SEVEN
The Youth Room

Gum in my carpet. Unbelievable. The lack of care is absurd. It's like they forget they are in a holy place. Which is maybe the point of this place. Attempting to make the whole Jesus situation more relatable to kids who have no desire to relate to anything older than them. I'm probably too harsh. I do see some teenager in the news every other day for getting accepted into med school or something crazy like that. I would prefer my doctor to go through puberty first, please. They do seem to evolve at speeds I can't keep up with. One day it's cool to drink cranberry juice, the next day there is a petition to free the cranberry farmers in a country I've never heard of. They are experts at moving fast and loud. It may not always be in the right direction, but at least there is movement back here. The folks in the front of the church could learn a thing or two about that. It gets a little stale up there. If any group of people in this church are going to shake things up it's going to be the kids back here still trying to figure out who they are. There will be some drama and some tears along with the juice, but that's better than a church thirsty for something to be passionate about.

This is a tough time of the year for them as well. The excitement for the first week of school has worn off and the realization of another difficult semester is settling into their souls. The slow days of summer seem to be fading from memory as the busy schedules packed full of basketball practices, garage-band riffs, and lunchtime-appointment fights take over. Jutte pool begins to clear out and the library welcomes back the familiar faces who forgot about it for the quick three-month sabbatical. Do kids still go to libraries? I remember when Suffolk used to hire us every other year for a big dusting. It was sad to see some of those books coated in such thick layers. My bookcase would never allow such disrespect. I may not open the books, but they are dust-free!

These are critical development years for these kids. If they visit this room at all that's a positive sign. I'm sure some are here by the nature of their parents' punishments, which seems to backfire just as much as it works as a corrective measure, but effort is always the first step. My parents didn't force me to go, so sharp attendance was never built in me. Besides, at their age parental pressure is never as strong as the peer type. Friends in church usually end in church. Friends in the street you can always meet. Dang. I should be a poet. It's true though. The words that come from the other people their age count three times as much as words coming from someone my age. That's true for the encouraging type and the more sinister kind. I gave out my fair share of both, but always knew when to stop. I never crossed the line. I don't know where that line is for them today, and I'm not sure they do either. That's what scares me. I hope their coaches and family members are pouring into them in the right ways.

DAY: TUESDAY, AUGUST 31
TIME: 10:44 A.M.
LOCATION: MINTERSON COUNTY POLICE STATION

No, no, no—Lord, not the school.

Protect everyone in those hallways right now. Let this be a false alarm or something.

Not in our town. Please, not in our town.

Source: Danielle Grainger, 33

DAY: WEDNESDAY, SEPTEMBER 1
TIME: 8:15 A.M.
LOCATION: ZEN BEDROOM

Father,

Today was supposed to be another regular Wednesday night. But today is anything but regular. Our community was rocked yesterday. I haven't felt that type of worry in years. I don't know what I would have done if we lost someone from our group. I'm not prepared for anything like that in my life right now, and I know these kids aren't. I know most of them, and the entire town, are in shock. Please guide us through this time as we recover from a scary day.

Finally, I still have to say I know we lost a soul yesterday, Lord. It may have been a soul that was long gone, but I know all life is precious to you. I hope people see that. I hope if there is anyone else out there hurting so bad that our church can reach them. That's why we are here—to introduce them to you so you can heal them before they turn down a dark path.

Thank you for the health of our kids and for your protection of our lives.

Amen.

Source: Wayne Zen, 35

DAY: THURSDAY, SEPTEMBER 2
TIME: 11:49 P.M.
LOCATION: FRANKLIN BEDROOM

God … I know I don't do what I'm supposed to. I know I don't pay attention or really care for all the religion in this town. But thank you for letting me wake up today. For me to be able to hug my parents and my siblings. What happened this week at school made me see I've been taking things for granted.

I mean … he was bleeding everywhere. There in the hallway, right where I walk every day. His family will never be the same. A lot of us might not be the same either. I don't want to be the same, I want to be better at being who you want me to be. I know it might take a lot of days to get there, but at least I have today. That's a start.

Thank you for today.

Source: Theresa Franklin, 16

DAY: FRIDAY, SEPTEMBER 3
TIME: 7:50 P.M.
LOCATION: GRANT BACKYARD

That will teach them, God.

That's why they can't take away our police and our guns: *they save lives*. If this wasn't a wake-up call to how everything they protest against is what keeps our country going, I don't know what is. You take away that officer and her gun and who knows how many kids that sicko would have mowed down. This could have been a tragedy if it wasn't for her courage. They want her to show up with some pepper spray and a psychology degree just to get gunned down. They don't understand that some people need to be put down; some people just can't be saved. You understand that.

You know people have to suffer the consequences of their actions. You are about true justice.

Thank you for that officer's courage. Thank you for our firearms and ability to protect ourselves.

Amen.

Source: Austin Grant, 58

Day: Saturday, September 4
Time: 11:37 a.m.
Location: Laslo Kitchen

This week was a nightmare.

I haven't been able to sleep since the shooting. What if that was outside my classroom? What if someone lost their life outside my door? How would I protect my kids?

I'm not built to handle a situation like that. I'm not built to be a protector. I'm an educator. If something happened to one of my students ... How did my workplace become a target for such evil?

Please look over these students who went through that traumatic experience. Protect their minds from that darkness.

Source: Bailey Laslo, 39

Day: Sunday, September 5
Time: 8:22 a.m.
Location: New Haven Backstage

Use me as best as you can today, Father. It's extremely evident this town needs you right now. They don't need me; they don't need doughnuts and coffee. They don't need high-quality production and catchy music people can clap their hands to. They don't need parking volunteers and greeters and worship staff and kids staff and day-care staff and more and more staff. They need you. They need you to still be in control of their lives. They need you to be bigger than any of their fears. They need you to bring them from this shadow over our community. Our community, state, and world are becoming murkier and murkier with selfish agendas, religious manipulation, coercive politics, and social-media-fueled lies that all add up to become powerful distractions to convince people you aren't who the word says you are. That you are not the great I Am. That you are not powerful enough to heal any lost soul. That you cannot bring people out of the darkness. That you do not represent hope. And when there is no hope in households ... well, you see how that trickles down into the minds of our youth and they take matters into their own hands. It's so devastating to see a child so lost and broken like that young boy. Right here in our community, within our reach. That's why this church is here; it's here for you to move through us and touch people like that young man. To save his life and every single person who doesn't know you.

Help us be the church people need right now. Help me deliver that message today.

Amen.

Source: Marcus Garland, 44

DAY: MONDAY, SEPTEMBER 6
TIME: 1:45 P.M.
LOCATION: RUDY'S PHARMACY

See, that kid needed some drugs. Drugs aren't all bad. They help us get through things. Cope with things. That's what they told me, now I'm still coping with the pain. The pain of the low.

I would have given that kid some drugs. Better to be addicted than to be dead ... or try to shoot up a school. I would never do anything like that; I could never hurt anyone. Only myself. It's okay to be selfish in that scenario, right?

Why is Rudy's closed? What's the point of this prescription if I can't use it? Where is Mr. Norman? I hope he isn't closing the joint. I'll keep him in business. I still need this place. I need these pills to keep the pain away. I need these pills to keep me away.

Source: Asher Sage, 38

DAY: TUESDAY, SEPTEMBER 7
TIME: 7:55 P.M.
LOCATION: CONCORD CONVENTION CENTER PARKING LOT

JESUS! HELP THESE PEOPLE! OPEN THEIR EYES SO THEY CAN WATCH THEMSELVES. WATCH YOUR BACKS. SATAN IS ALWAYS RIGHT AROUND THE CORNER. TURN TO GOD BEFORE IT IS TOO LATE! TURN TO GOD BEFORE YOU TURN THE CORNER AND FIND SATAN WAITING TO STEAL, KILL, AND DESTROY EVERYTHING THAT YOU HOLD DEAR.

I WARNED YOU! I TOLD YOU WHAT WAS COMING OF THIS WORLD. CHILDREN WHO ONLY KNOW HOW TO SPEAK WITH PHONES AND GUNS. RIGHT HERE IN OUR OWN TOWN. YOU THINK THE EVIL IS FAR AWAY BUT IT'S RIGHT HERE. IT'S YOUR NEIGHBORS. IT'S YOUR FRIENDS AND FAMILY. THEY ARE THE ONES WHO MUST BE WATCHED!

SAVE YOURSELF!

Source: Verl Muncy, 63

Day: Wednesday, September 8
Time: 4:00 a.m.
Location: Byrdwood Garage

God, I know the whole town is fine with that boy not making it, but I still don't feel right about it.

He was clearly suffering mentally, and he clearly needed someone to tell him that. With these skills you have given me, I can save lives and perform amazing feats, but I can't fix a brain that isn't viewing the world around it in the proper frame. That's not my specialty.

I know the chances of me saving him when he was brought in were practically zero, but I've made those work before. I wanted to save him so that you could *really* save him. Everyone thinks death equals closure, but it doesn't. His family will live on with the legacy of their son. That officer will move on in her career with this asterisk on her resume. There is very little redemption in this story.

Source: Percy Byrdwood, 50

Day: Friday, September 10
Time: 10:38 p.m.
Location: Saltwater Hall A Mackenzie College Room 205

I miss home already.

This doesn't feel like my team, my coaches, my friends, any of that. Did I make a mistake?

Maybe I need to be patient. That was never my strength back home, but there I knew I could go get what I wanted and knew how to make it happen. Here, I don't even know how to get to my classes.

Give me the patience to stick through this first semester and see what happens. Help me step out of my comfort zone and open myself up to people.

Source: Layla Sacron, 17

DAY: SATURDAY, SEPTEMBER 11
TIME: 11:17 A.M.
LOCATION: BANKS LAWN

Well, we've just about made it through, God.

No miracles this summer, just more backbreaking work and sweat. Lots and lots of sweat. You'd think I'd be in better shape after each summer but, yet, here I am, still soft in the belly and flabby in the arms trying to make our own yard look pristine. It doesn't really matter though, the boss will come home and do it over again just to make a point. What a guy. I wonder what kind of childhood trauma he went through to make me work like this. I never hear him talk about his dad or what they used to do together. I wish I could have met Grandpa before he died. I bet he wouldn't make me work like this in the summer. Or he would at least buy me one of those hat umbrellas to protect me from the sun and all its evil ways.

Thanks for another summer that flew by and for no rocks breaking windows or blades being bent. The real summer miracle.

Source: Elliott Banks, 15

DAY: SUNDAY, SEPTEMBER 12
TIME: 3:38 P.M.
LOCATION: BANKS LAWN

He may not see it now, but these are the summers he'll appreciate when he's older and has responsibilities bigger than proper grass patterns in life.

If anything, I'm thankful for these summers I get to spend with him. How I get to watch him grow up and give him everything my dad didn't pass down to me. I know I never appreciated the little time I had with my dad, but even when he was around he never opened up to me. I don't know if it was my mom and the energy

she brought to the home or something that I could have fixed ...
but I hope my son feels more love around him than I ever did. The
summers we share together now will be gone before he knows it.
I don't want him to feel like I didn't try to teach him everything I
know. Half of it he won't care about for ten years, but at least I can
go to bed knowing I said what I needed to say.

I pray he's learning more than he leads on. I hope he's better
equipped for life than I was.

Source: Gavin Banks, 46

DAY: MONDAY, SEPTEMBER 13
TIME: 11:48 P.M.
LOCATION: KING$ DREAM STUDIO

I've missed this place. It's been too long, too much time between
sessions for this to feel like home.

That's what I'm afraid of, that each day not following this dream
is a day wasted on vapors. I know the things of this world will fade
away quickly, that's why I want to create something that is bigger
than me, something that will live on forever, like you.

How do you do it? How do you create something that is
thousands of years old but still relevant today? Is it foolish of me to
think I can make something like that? You used humans who were
broken, in prison, fearful, and far from you to create words that
breathe life. So why can't you use me?

Source: Booker Naheem, 22

DAY: TUESDAY, SEPTEMBER 14
TIME: 4:44 P.M.
LOCATION: SUFFOLK PUBLIC LIBRARY

As always, she cares too much. But I see it now.

I wasn't subbing at the school when everything went down, and she was still the first to text and check in on me. Shoot, Dad barely even knew anything happened at school and was more surprised the cop was a woman than anything else.

I guess all the pressure of being the responsible one in the house has fallen on her shoulders. Still, I wish she didn't worry so much. Isn't there some verse you have about being anxious? That's what I should do, start sending her Bible verses that she can't be mad about because they are spot on.

I'm humbled by her constant care for me, God. I hope I care about someone that much one day.

Source: Leo Haranna, 37

DAY: WEDNESDAY, SEPTEMBER 15
TIME: 10:05 P.M.
LOCATION: GARLAND BEDROOM

Please don't let my parents pull me out of school, God.

I know what happened at the school was scary, but scary things happen every day. Homeschooling me isn't the answer. That will ruin my life. I'll be a walking stereotype at that point.

The more they try to control every little facet of my life the more I want to find a new family. All this "family name" and "take pride in what we are doing as a family" talk doesn't change the fact that I see their imperfections every day, and everyone thinks we are a perfect family or something.

I wish we could be ourselves. You'll love us no matter what. I know that much.

Source: Jonah Garland, 16

DAY: THURSDAY, SEPTEMBER 16
TIME: 12:28 P.M.
LOCATION: BERTON DOG PARK

I see why Salem has been acting short in our meetings now. That's terrible news about Izzy. I wonder how many people know. The Faulkners are such great parents. I've never seen them look so ... shaken.

This is a chance for me to do what I love and support my students outside of the flash cards and study techniques. Help me support Salem and their entire family as they work through this.

Source: Angel Zombuka, 28

DAY: FRIDAY, SEPTEMBER 17
TIME: 8:52 P.M.
LOCATION: CLAREMORE BUS STATION

Jesus, I'm open to ideas. I'm all ears on how we can survive and live by your standards. But right now, I don't see it.

I feel like my entire life I've had to make decisions between bad and worse. When is the breakthrough? When do things turn around for the little people of the world who start with nothing and end with nothing plus a dollar? Heck, a dollar isn't even enough for me to get to work at the Tooney's place. Why do they live so far away from everything? I guess that's what you do when you have so much, keep it far from everyone else. Their excess covers up my guilt some, but I still don't love my actions out there. They pay me well to help take care of their livestock and land, but not enough to keep me from the occasional pull from the purse. Too trusting, I guess.

I can't let my little boy grow up in this. He deserves so much more. Take all my blessings and give them to him. Let him be the one who makes the leap forward in our family. Shine bright on him.

Source: Toni Gentle, 39

DAY: SATURDAY, SEPTEMBER 18
TIME: 1:50 P.M.
LOCATION: HAMMY'S DRIVE-THRU

Can't his mom take my side one time?

I'm getting drained from being the one who's always in the doghouse. The one who always has to sacrifice. The one who can't take the promotion in a different state. The one who comes in with the wrong tone.

This partnership is starting to mirror a war, and I can only handle losing so many battles.

Source: Kenny Sturgiss, 38

DAY: SUNDAY, SEPTEMBER 19
TIME: 3:39 P.M.
LOCATION: WALLARD BEDROOM

I feel like I've aged four years in the past four weeks. Is that what old feels like? I don't like it.

If this is the beginning of the end for me, at least let me go out in style. I need my final-day outfit looking nice and tight on these saggy bones. My funeral needs to be a festival. Those folks better be weeping is all I know. Harrison will pour one out for me. What are we gonna do with him? That young man needs someone to look out for him. He needs a proper woman in his life, not someone three times his age like me. I wonder why he's single. He's young, handsome, and Black. My mom would have rolled over in her grave if I ever. What an amazing thought.

Source: Harriett Wallard, 92

DAY: MONDAY, SEPTEMBER 20
TIME: 7:32 A.M.
LOCATION: VERDANA KITCHEN

Thank you for today, this week, this month, and this entire year, God. I've come so far and I'm still not done.

I never knew how much a change on the outside would create a change on the inside for me. That's what I love the most about this year: my entire perspective on life has been changed. The frame in what I see as possible versus what is out of my reach has expanded so much.

With what I've been able to accomplish this year, I know anything is possible with you by my side.

Source: Bri Verdana, 30

DAY: TUESDAY, SEPTEMBER 21
TIME: 2:02 P.M.
LOCATION: SILENT NIGHT COFFEE SHOP

Let this plan work. Give me the courage to take these steps. This is the only way out I see. Give me and my baby girl protection on this journey we are about to embark on. I know it won't be easy, but this is the way toward a better life. I feel it.

Watch over all my babies I'm leaving behind at the church. I know you'll look over them. Give them my warmth. Let them know Auntie Palmy will always be praying for them.

Source: Beiba Palmandi, 45

DAY: WEDNESDAY, SEPTEMBER 22
TIME: 5:42 P.M.
LOCATION: CLAREMORE BUS-STATION BENCH

I thought you controlled the storms? I thought the seas beckoned to your will?

What did I do for you to leave me in the storm? Do I belong in the valley? Was I so arrogant on the mountaintop that the valley is where I belong now? Every time I take a step toward pulling things together—just a night in a motel—I'm struck by fate, or you, or the devil himself.

The light is truly starting to dim on me. I see less and less reason for me to still act like you are out there and have some grand plan for my life. I refuse to believe this is what you want for me.

Source: Ulises Zind, 41

DAY: THURSDAY, SEPTEMBER 23
TIME: 6:58 A.M.
LOCATION: CURTIS KITCHEN

Lord, please help Graham get on board with the plan. I don't know why he's being hesitant. I can see it in his eyes and his mannerisms. He doesn't want to say it because he's too nice; I've always been the more direct out of us two, and now his indecision is slowing us down. Each day that goes by hurts our chances to make all of this happen.

I know this is a lot, but this is what we have to do now. This isn't the way I wanted it to be, but I'm here for it and I'm here to make it work. Help him get there. Help my hubby help me.

The joy of our future child will be better than anything we are going through right now. I know that much is true.

Source: Tricia Curtis, 32

Day: Friday, September 24
Time: 11:35 a.m.
Location: Brooklyn Prep Elementary School

It's been too long, God. I know my parents are trying to hide the truth from me, but I looked up the stats online. It said after two weeks the likelihood of her coming back goes way down. I don't want that to be true, but I can't shake the feeling that she's gone forever. She was the best thing about the entire year. The house is so quiet now. We couldn't stand her farts but at least she kept everyone laughing. I miss her so much.

Did you put her in my life just to take her from me? No way. Please bring her back. I know she's out there somewhere. She's probably waiting on us to come save her.

Amen.

Source: Miles Branch, 10

DAY: SATURDAY, SEPTEMBER 25
TIME: 10:33 A.M.
LOCATION: KINGSTON JUVENILE CENTER

Lord, before we start today, please open the ears of these young men in front of me so they walk away from this conversation with the knowledge that you are the way, the truth, and the life and that you alone have the power to save and transform their lives. I know they see me as some old man who lost his edge behind bars, but in reality, I gained something so much sweeter when I found you. I found a meaning to my life that no one could take away. Not the law, the police, the government, or the person who signs my paycheck; you are higher than all of those things. I hope these men can see that. I hope they see that by serving you they can find fulfillment in something that is eternal versus something that will be gone tomorrow.

Speak through me as we talk today, and come into this room and bless us with your presence. I thank you for this time we are allotted, and let us not waste it.

In your name we pray, amen.

Source: Oscar Abbernathy, 61

DAY: MONDAY, SEPTEMBER 27
TIME: 6:18 P.M.
LOCATION: QUINO BACKYARD

I'm so ashamed. I finally had a chance to do the right thing and I clearly fucked it up. Maybe I should have told my brother about my conversations with Ronnie. Or maybe that would have made it worse, if that's possible. But how could they say that on TV? That they are "accepting all thoughts and prayers in this tough time." Somehow, they made their son's death about them. Somehow, they are accepting pity for being the terrible parents who raised a kid as sick as Ronnie.

I don't understand how he snuck a gun in and out of their home. Their house "under God's guidance," as they liked to say. Well, I guess I do. If it's not up to their standards they don't look at it, just like they never looked at Ronnie. The real Ronnie. The Taylor Swift fan. The sneaky-good bowler. The young boy who will now never get the chance to become an old man. I hate to admit I'm relieved those other kids will get the chance to grow old now. It hurts to think what Ronnie could have done. And it hurts even more to think this was just his way out. His way to go out being seen. Being known.

But that seems to be the lesser of the evils here. I pray that Ronnie was never going to use that gun. That he wanted to be stopped before he hurt himself or anyone. At least give me that.

Source: Wesley Quino, 40

DAY: TUESDAY, SEPTEMBER 28
TIME: 9:05 A.M.
LOCATION: GRACE JENKINS CHILDREN'S HOSPITAL

I don't know how to feel. I don't know how we are supposed to act like everything is fine when it isn't.

Everything else matters so little right now. I can't think about tomorrow, next month, or next year when we need a miracle *today*. Each day the doctors come in here and tell us to stay positive and to keep our heads up, but then tell us things don't look good. Do they not see the dissonance?

I hate feeling like I can't solve this for her. I've been able to fix everything for her before this. She'll never see me the same once this is all done. Because I still believe this is going to be all over at one point, we just need it to be sooner rather than later.

Source: Michael Faulkner, 37

DAY: WEDNESDAY, SEPTEMBER 29
TIME: 8:18 P.M.
LOCATION: TOONEY FARMS

What happened at the school this month is exactly why I know I'm supposed to give away our land for the city's future.

Our community needs resources, buildings, employees, and spaces for people who need help like that young man. I hope the shelters, health services, and housing the city plans to create with our gift will see the light of day. He is the type of person I feel responsible to help with everything you've given our family. I don't know if we could have changed his future, or anyone's involved in that terrible incident, but we have to try. We have to, right? This can't be all in vain, can it?

I can't believe you blessed us like this for us to simply enjoy these blessings. You fill our cup so we can fill others. Help us be generous with your eternal cup.

Source: Fallon Tooney, 71

DAY: THURSDAY, SEPTEMBER 30
TIME: 7:48 P.M.
LOCATION: NEW HAVEN BREAKOUT ROOM

God,

Help me get through these meetings with these weirdos. I mean, do I really seem as messed up as the rest of these folks? That one girl—Jessica I think they called her—she has crazy all in her eyes. Beard man with tattoos looks like he just got done choppin' up some bodies. Buddy with the unpronounceable name legit has one arm. And Chelsea, the ringleader of them all, I know she means good, but she's—a lot. Always trying to trap me after the meetings and chat me up like we have anything in common, besides the fact that at one time she was apparently jacked up like the rest of us. I would have liked to meet the old version of her. I bet she was fun.

Help me slide in and out of these meetings with as little attention as possible. And if you could get us the good doughnuts from the place on Cherry that would be fantastic.

Source: Zayn Niro, 44

DAY: SATURDAY, OCTOBER 2
TIME: 11:22 P.M.
LOCATION: RUDY'S PHARMACY

Look at me, Lord, you have me tearing up in my own store, scaring away customers probably—ha. I'll call these my joyful allergy tears. I can appreciate everything you've provided for my family through this store. As much as I hate to see this stage come to an end, I know it's time to trust in you. You are bigger than any financial strategy or five-year plan.

I wouldn't want it any other way. My children were able to see us do good by the people around us and help many of them through serious pain and the occasional seasonal allergy. If I was able to teach them anything I pray they learned that whatever we bring to the table is multiplied and expanded when it's touched by you, so they might as well bring everything to you first and watch you work.

Please help me stay in the present and enjoy these last few Saturdays I have in this version of my business baby with these strangers who have become friends after all these years.

And keep these "allergies" under control.

Amen.

Source: Rudy Norman, 38

Day: Sunday, October 3
Time: 2:45 p.m.
Location: Freedom Basketball Courts

God, why don't I feel like I did when I got back from camp this summer? When I got back I felt like—like I was more aware of your presence around me. I felt like I could tell what you wanted my mind to focus on and my heart to move toward.

I know I've gotten back into some bad habits, but I don't feel the guilt of them like I did this summer. Is it this easy to drift away from you?

I don't want to drift away. Help me feel the push of your guidance in the right direction—even when my feet are stuck in the sand. I don't want to go back to when I didn't feel remorse for anything I did. That was a dangerous place to be.

Source: Zehare Joyce, 16

Day: Monday, October 4
Time: 9:50 a.m.
Location: Furtan Mailbox

I can't let my parents see these bills that come in, Jesus. The hospital looked at me crazy when I asked to have all the bills sent in the mail, but I can't risk them opening their emails or mine and seeing these dollar amounts. They'd freak out and start yelling around the house asking why you cursed our family. I still don't know how I'm going to pay them. I'm still not even back to 100 percent and they don't want me back to work if I can't move like I used to. I'm sure they've already given my job to the "next man up" anyway. Next man up is great when you're the next man up. It sucks when you're the one who made the hole to fill.

Dr. Byrdwood was nice enough to meet with me after church and walk me through some of those rehab movements and drills so I didn't have to waste time and more money paying for physical therapy, but I'm not sure it's enough. I got a little limp now when I wake up in the morning ... and I'm not street enough to walk with a limp for the rest of my life.

We need a miracle for those bills, Jesus. That's the only way I see it.

Source: Benny Furtan, 22

Day: Tuesday, October 5
Time: 11:30 p.m.
Location: Fermington Bathroom

This is a nightmare. Now they're trying to make the band work with no front man? Everything's gonna fall apart—all the momentum we had, all the synergy we were building—just because I was too prideful and now they are too prideful about letting me back in.

Can't they see that's the only way it can get back to normal? Our chemistry was off the charts, and our future songs were gonna top the charts. We had the *it* factor.

I don't know what else I can do, God. The only one who will answer my snaps is Sessy, and she's afraid Margarette will get mad at her if she says anything about me.

Save our band. Do whatever it takes, God.

Amen.

Source: Trevor Fermington, 17

DAY: THURSDAY, OCTOBER 7
TIME: 10:49 A.M.
LOCATION: SALTWATER HALL A MACKENZIE COLLEGE ROOM 101

Father, please look over Layla. I worry for all my freshmen, but I can tell she is having serious trouble.

You know I don't do the whole sport thing, so I have trouble connecting with her, but I can tell she wants and needs someone to talk to. Help her open up to me and feel safe sharing with me. She seems like the type who had it all together in high school and got to college and got her shit rocked by a few hard months.

Good thing we have you to lean on. I saw her eyes light up when I mentioned the women's Bible study starting next semester, so let's hope she makes it that far.

The first semester is always the worst. Thank you for putting me here right now for these freshies, and help me be a source of peace and confidence in their lives.

Source: Kamden Upstin, 19

DAY: FRIDAY, OCTOBER 8
TIME: 7:07 A.M.
LOCATION: MANY MEN BIBLE STUDY (CHAUCER KITCHEN)

We believe in the power of praying as a church, and we want to put action behind those words in this time we spend together each Friday, Lord. So we continue to lift up Michael and his family as they look for you to do the work only you can do and provide his little chica with a miracle. We pray that you give Michael the strength to be the leader in his household and guide his family through these turbulent waters. We know nothing is impossible to you and we ask for grace and mercy to shower over the Faulkner family as they need every ounce of support we can offer right now. Help us love them as you would.

We accept that your ways are higher than ours and your knowledge is beyond measure; we are thankful to surrender to such a powerful God and give our lives to you.

Thank you for each moment we are able to spend together and gather in your name.

Amen.

Source: Keith Chaucer, 35

DAY: SATURDAY, OCTOBER 9
TIME: 4:15 P.M.
LOCATION: CLAREMORE BUS STATION

Why did I just laugh at that "gay" joke that man made on the bus? Do I hate who I am that much?

That's it, I'm done, God. I'm over all of this. Before the end of the year, it's gonna happen.

I'm gonna be who you made me to be and love you as you called me to. I can do both.

Source: Dustin Saudiner, 21

DAY: SUNDAY, OCTOBER 10
TIME: 8:44 A.M.
LOCATION: NEW HAVEN STAGE

Father, we praise you for the opportunity to give back to your church that has done so much more than we could ever repay. We don't look at our tithes and offerings as a burden, but as a gift to give back to you and put you in control of our finances. We know you can do more with 10 percent than we could ever do with the rest, so we lift it all up to you and believe in your power to multiply and make whole that which appears to be "not enough" in our eyes. You are more than enough in all areas of our lives, and that includes our checkbooks, so let us remain committed to building your kingdom and supporting the good works you are able to achieve through us here on Earth.

We give glory to you in all that we do, and everybody said: Amen.

Source: Marcus Garland, 44

Day: Monday, October 11
Time: 9:50 P.M.
Location: Metzen Bathroom

Lord, please help Kenny and Hauz figure this out. I can't go through another difficult separation. I told myself the last one was the last one. If I can't get a man to accept me and my son and get on the same page with us, then maybe love isn't in the cards for me. Kenny seemed like he was ready, at least he convinced me he was. And I know Hauz can be a lot and he doesn't make it easy, but they have to get on the same page. This tension in the house is not how I want my son growing up. I want better for him than what I had.

I have no more tricks; I have no more books to read. All I have is you.

I can only stand this for so much longer. I'm exhausted from being their mediator and peacemaker. Why are the men in my life so stubborn?

Source: Penelope Metzen, 40

Day: Tuesday, October 12
Time: 6:35 a.m.
Location: Grainger Kitchen

Give me the confidence to do this job as best as I can, God.

Give me the courage that Margarie had that day in the school. I don't know if I would have been able to do what she did and take that shot, but she did the right thing. But ever since she became the hero she rightfully deserves to be, I've really doubted myself. I've never had an issue with comparing myself to other people, I've always compared myself to who you want me to be, but this feeling is nauseating. I'm ... unsure. And I hate it. I've always been the girl who believes in herself, like, I'm badass. With you by my side, I've conquered everything in front of me. School. Tests. The academy. Misogyny. I'm the person I would have looked up to fifteen years ago. But does any of that matter if I can't make it happen in the heat of the moment?

Put my feet on solid ground, God. Put that fire back in me to believe I'm everything I seem to be.

Source: Danielle Grainger, 33

CHAPTER EIGHT
The Offices

I swear eyes are following you when you walk around back here. Someone's right behind you making sure you don't open any drawers or glance at any notebooks too long. Not that I would want to do anything like that, but it does make you wonder what kind of secrets are kept back here. This is where the dirty robes get straightened out and pressed clean for the next weekend. Where the unholy talks take place. Money talk never feels as clean as it should be. Even when dollars are being put into the charity bucket, there is still a hint of doubt in the air. Should the money be going somewhere else? Is it worth it to keep putting money into the never-ending well of the "community"? Those are the questions I ask myself with my few bucks tossed into the bin every other month, so I can only imagine what the conversations with the whole pie must be like. Marcus always puts on a good smile and is joyful for the church's generosity to the kingdom. But he has to say that contractually, pretty sure. And that worship pastor. Sheesh. He likes to beat it into people too. I like him more when he is strumming the guitar than taking a hold of the mic for a second. Leave that to the professionals, buddy.

There are more than safes to vacuum around back here, though, there is this lost and found that never shrinks. How can you forget your shoes in the church? I know a few homeless folks who would appreciate these sneaks. Even Mr. Street Pastor would take some of this stuff. Heck, I could use this rain jacket. I bet they hold on to it just in case the visitor comes back so they can wow them with superior customer service. That's a good description for back here: Customer Service Department. Where everyone submits their complaints and shares their thoughts and opinions around how the business should *really* be run. I mean church. I bet the leadership team loves those emails and phone calls. Unfortunately, they don't have the luxury of being okay with losing a few customers to yearly attrition. I'd be happy to put in a few hours on the lines to filter incoming calls. I'd take the bad reviews to give them a break and only let the good calls past the gate. I'm good at letting people get their grievances out and sending them right through the old noggin into nothingness. Years of practice with my first wife on that one. The ratio between compliment and complaint would be a lovely number to see. Marcus should start the next service with that number on the screen and drop the mic. I'd show up early for that type of confrontational preaching. Imagine that: showing up early to church. I know these offices come alive at dawn with the hustle and bustle of the leadership types. Lots of early-morning anxiety and stress moving through the vents back here. That's why I always leave some friendly scents around. The right smell to start the day can change your outlook on life. Just ask bacon.

DAY: THURSDAY, OCTOBER 14
TIME: 8:45 P.M.
LOCATION: NEW HAVEN OFFICES

Why do we make it so easy for people to give online now? I know you're a cash guy, God. Cash is king and you're King and yeah, yeah, all that good stuff that Marcus likes to preach. We'll see how convincing his tithing prayer was this week.

I know he doesn't like praying over the tithe, that's why he always lets some other "elder" come up and pray over it. At least I can do it with a level of earnestness knowing that I'll be coming right back here to the safe to get out a few dollars. I see it as my end-of-quarter bonus. If only Marcus would let us pay ourselves a living wage. He's so stingy with it all. Can't he see we are growing like crazy and deserve some pay increases? I've been singing my lungs out. That should earn me something, but noooo, everything needs to be reinvested to "grow our presence in the city." I get tired of him being so holy all the time. He's never had to struggle. He's never had to go through what I'm going through. Look at me, pulling pennies out of the bucket for my pill habit. Pennies for pills … pennies for pills … pennies for pills.

Yeah, seriously, God, help our congregation give more money. Preferably in cash.

Source: Asher Sage, 38

DAY: FRIDAY, OCTOBER 15
TIME: 8:37 A.M.
LOCATION: CROOKED HEIGHTS HIGH SCHOOL FOOTBALL OFFICES

I pray for Daxon and his knee right now, Father. This is what I hate to see; this is why I'm so hard on them in the weight room. I'm trying to build their bodies up to withstand the intensity of this beautiful game. I'm sick today—last night's game was perfect except for that.

Daxon has such a bright future. I hope he keeps his head up and knows we'll get him through this. That he can come back even better than before.

Lead him to a fast recovery and a return like never before. Most of all I pray that he knows that no matter his status or ability to play that he is loved by all of his teammates and coaches.

Source: Oliver Pernell, 48

DAY: SATURDAY, OCTOBER 16
TIME: 7:45 A.M.
LOCATION: HANOI PLAYROOM

Good morning, Mr. Christ. It's a great Saturday today, and I think you know why.

Today is the season premiere of my show. I've patiently waited all summer for its return and it's finally here.

With today being such an important day, I was hoping you could seal a few things up for me. First, no interruptions from my sister. No play talk, no "help me build" whatever, no time for those things this morning. Second, my parents. Let this be a sleepy Saturday for them so they don't wake up with a lengthy list of chores that they could easily do themselves.

Lastly, our neighbor's dog. It hurts to see Miles so sad about his dog being gone. You know I have no need for a slobbery dog jumping all over me, but he loved that dog. I hope he finds it.

Oh, but really really last, I hope this season is amazing.

Amen.

Source: Victor Hanoi, 8

Day: Monday, October 18
Time: 4:14 P.M.
Location: Camden First Bank

We need the end-of-year push. Really bad, God. Marcus can stay positive, but I'm a realist. Put that old giving spirit in the congregation, Lord. Do what only you can do.

Source: Emory Garland, 48

Day: Tuesday, October 19
Time: 4:18 P.M.
Location: Macary Park Creek

Was this dumb dog supposed to be your birthday present for me?

Now, when I can't even save my own life, you want me to help preserve the life of this animal who probably ran away from a good life with people who loved her, who took care of all her needs, shared their space with her, spent money on her well-being, and she threw it all away. When she ran up on me, she was cleaner than me. A few weeks go by and now she fits in—like someone who belongs in the streets. Maybe she was always destined to run away from everything life gave her. Guess she really is like me then.

Source: Ulises Zind, 42

Day: Wednesday, October 20
Time: 11:24 a.m.
Location: Grace Jenkins Children's Hospital Cafeteria

I've said it every way I know how, God: we need a miracle. I've prayed, and I've prayed, and I've prayed some more. I've been to prayer groups and prayer groups have specifically been made for me now, and ... silence. Well, worse than silence, it's deterioration. It's the opposite of what's supposed to come of our resiliency and our belief in our faith in you.

Sometimes I don't think this is about us, like this is some cruel show our church is watching on how a family is supposed to go through a tragedy like this. Like this is practice for them on how to be a church family and support someone in the tribe who's hurting. For some reason, though, my gut is telling me I won't be able to take the ending.

Source: Roxy Faulkner, 38

Day: Friday, October 22
Time: 6:35 p.m.
Location: The Vista Shopping Center

LORD! HELP YOUR FLOCK KEEP THEIR EYES OPEN!

THE SINISTER ONE WILL BE HIDING IN PLAIN SIGHT NEXT WEEK. HE WILL MASK HIMSELF AMONG THE COMMON PEOPLE. HE WILL COME TO STEAL YOUR SOUL IN THE QUIET OF NIGHT.

YOU ALL INVITE HIM INTO YOUR LIVES. YOU DRESS UP AS HIM AND ACT LIKE HE IS JUST A BAD PERSON. NO! HE IS THE FALLEN ONE. THE ONE WHO LED ADAM AND EVE ASTRAY. HE WANTS TO BRING SHAME TO YOUR LIFE.

BE CAREFUL. BE CAUTIOUS. WATCH THOSE CLOSE TO YOU TO MAKE SURE THEY DO NOT FALL AS WELL. TURN TO THE LORD AND AWAY FROM THE DEVIL!

Source: Verl Muncy, 63

Day: Saturday, October 23
Time: 9:41 p.m.
Location: Grace Jenkins Memorial Hospital

Lord, thank you for another day to come in here and do what you made me to do. Thank you for putting people like Mrs. Wallard in my path. That's what I love the most about my job: meeting all of these amazing people who have traveled the world and have accumulated these stories of life and love and loss. Yes, a lot of them come in sick or in pain or some just barely agitated, but I love the responsibility of being the one who can help them get back to creating a life full of stories—and Mrs. Wallard is one of those characters who is never short of a great story. She seemed a few steps slower this time around, though. I know she's eager to get on to the next phase of existence but at our last checkup she had too much sass in here to be ready to go. This time she seemed a little tired. A little ... over it all.

No matter what, I hope Mrs. Wallard is either telling stories down here or with you and the rest of the angels up in heaven.

Source: Percy Byrdwood, 50

DAY: SUNDAY, OCTOBER 24
TIME: 9:39 A.M.
LOCATION: TARGET AISLE 5

This is what you want me to be able to do, eh, Jesus? Afford the good cereal from Target for my kid, right? Does my kid not deserve nice things?

He is such a good little boy. I don't want him growing up thinking we are too poor for the good cereal. I know how growing up in poverty makes you think. It makes you think the world isn't made for you. It makes you second-guess every step and every promise of something brighter in your future. It's a cloud hanging right over your shoulder. I can't let that happen to him.

I'll take whatever future punishments I'm due for my actions as long as he is set up to succeed in life. That starts with the name-brand cereal to start his days.

Source: Toni Gentle, 39

DAY: MONDAY, OCTOBER 25
TIME: 10:02 P.M.
LOCATION: HARANNA BEDROOM

Him moving out has been wonderful, no need to act like that isn't true, God, but I worry about him. What happened at the school scared me more than him. What if someone broke into his house while he was asleep? He sleeps like a bear, and I know he isn't locking his doors. I at least have Dad here to snore intruders away.

For some reason I miss him more than I thought I would. I guess a part of me got used to taking care of him. He balanced me out too. All my anxiety was fine when there was someone else around for me to be anxious about. Now I'm anxious about myself—and it's not a cute look.

I pray that you ease my mind and heart and constantly remind me that there is no need to worry when you take care of the flowers in the field.

Source: Estella Haranna, 40

Day: Wednesday, October 27
Time: 6:16 a.m.
Location: The Rack (Athletics Weight Room) Mackenzie College

Thank you for this amazing game, God. For the game that has given me more than I could ever give it. I love it so much … and I don't understand why it isn't loving me back right now.

I've never felt like this on a team before. I've never been "just another girl" on the team. I know I'm working as hard as I always have, but now it's not enough all of a sudden. It doesn't help that our upperclassmen look at me as a threat instead of a teammate to help make us better. It's wack for them to be like that, and it's wack for me to let it get to me.

My game used to do the talking for me, but now I feel like I've lost my voice.

Source: Layla Sacron, 18

DAY: THURSDAY, OCTOBER 28
TIME: 9:37 P.M.
LOCATION: HOLIDAY MOVIE ROOM

Please help my parents stay together, Jesus.

I know they've been trying to hide it for some time now, and half of me wants them to be happy and to stop fighting—but that would only come from spending a lot less time around each other. Like, none.

Half of my friends' parents are already divorced, and they act like it's fine, but I know it isn't. I know how messy everything can be. I'm really, really worried about Jamie. He's too young to understand what a divorce would be like. What if they tried to split us up? Dad wouldn't let me go with Mom, but Jamie is such a momma's boy.

I can't think about any of this ... just fix my parents, please, Jesus.

Source: Nasir Holiday, 14

DAY: FRIDAY, OCTOBER 29
TIME: 3:18 P.M.
LOCATION: KINGSTON JUVENILE CENTER

Father, we thank you for being a just and merciful Lord. We know our actions require certain consequences, and we pray that you use those consequences to transform our hearts toward ones that are on fire for you. We have all made mistakes, and we have all done things that earned us the reward of death, but you have conquered death and that is reason to rejoice every day. You defeated death and have given us another life to live through you. I pray that each young man here realizes how sweet it is to live a life that is guided by you. This world is constantly changing, and what's right one day seems to be wrong the next, but you remain the same today, tomorrow, and forever. I hope this truth gives these men hope in something to build the foundation of their lives on. I know my life balanced out when I relied on you and not on my own strength or knowledge.

Let us praise you with our focus and dedication to your word and to each other.

In your name we pray, amen.

Source: Oscar Abbernathy, 61

Day: Saturday, October 30
Time: 6:22 p.m.
Location: Lansing Kitchen

I know it's nights like these that can get crazy, Father, so please keep a special eye out for Maleek. Take care of my g-baby ... tell him that I love him and I'll never stop praying for him.

Tell him there is always space for him next to me. He doesn't have to be ashamed about anything.

Tell him your love is greater than any failure.

Source: Gigi Lansing, 83

Day: Sunday, October 31
Time: 4:01 p.m.
Location: CVS on Omaha

My first piece of candy this year? I think so!

God—thank you for chocolate and all of its magical powers.

Source: Bri Verdana, 30

DAY: MONDAY, NOVEMBER 1
TIME: 2:45 P.M.
LOCATION: HAMPTON MALL

Allllright now, God, how about that game yesterday? That was somethin' wild. They must feed these fellows somethin' different nowadays. They weren't moving so fast back when I played. I wouldn't have made it past third grade with how good these kids look now.

I'm just happy I made it through with no injuries. No broken skulls or concussions ... that I know of. I worry about my grandkids out there now running around. I told their mom that they should have played baseball. The sport is so violent—too violent for some little tykes who can barely walk in a straight line with no helmet or pads on. But no, they "want to be like Grandpa." I don't want them to be like me, I want them to be better than me. I want to see them grow up to do great things. I'm afraid I'm going to miss out on their lives.

Keep me around long enough to at least see some Friday-night lights.

Source: Prentice Truth, 77

Day: Tuesday, November 2
Time: 7:21 A.M.
Location: Saudiner Half Bath

I know, I've been living in fear all year. I'm afraid that he's going to push me away if I confront him about it. Well, I don't want it to be a confrontation, I want it to be a conversation that brings back his smile. That brings back all the beautiful things about him. I know he's being shackled by these chains holding him down. This chain's telling him that he'll lose us if he reveals the truth.

Please show him I already know the truth and I'm still right here.

Source: Everett Saudiner, 28

Day: Thursday, November 4
Time: 11:50 A.M.
Location: Lowe's Parking Lot

I forgot how fulfilling starting over can be. It's been so long since I had to roll up my sleeves and go to Lowe's and spend time in the paint aisle. I didn't know there were so many different shades of red, but I found the perfect hue.

Thank you for this opportunity to start again. For putting my family around me through this time and for the clarity to see what the pharmacy can be turned in to. By myself everything seems too large to overcome, but with you I know anything can be done.

Guide our steps as my family and I start this new chapter of life, Lord.

Source: Rudy Norman, 38

DAY: FRIDAY, NOVEMBER 5
TIME: 9:15 P.M.
LOCATION: JOYCE BEDROOM

It's been a long year, Lord, and it's still not over yet. I know we go through seasons close to you and far from you, so I pray that this is a season for Zehare to be in your embrace.

I knew the post-hype excitement of the camp would cool off, but I still see a change in my boy. It can be hard to maintain that desire for you, I know that—there have been plenty of times in my life where I didn't go to you first about anything. But I ask that you keep Zehare close to you in these final months of the year. Help him end the year in a season of prayer and commitment to you. Help him make time for you in his daily schedule.

Thank you for the highs and lows of life and for making everything work according to your will.

Amen.

Source: Helena Joyce, 41

CHAPTER NINE
The Lobby

The crown jewel in the queen's headpiece. Where smiles are served up on pretty platters and hands are shaken with eagerness. Eager to come back or eager to leave? That's the question. Amazingly, this place is always the easiest to clean for me. There are so many eyes examining every square inch in here that the members usually do their part and keep it tidy enough for visitors. The trash is supervised so it never gets too full. A full trash can sends the wrong vibes, which is a good bit of sanitation irony. If the trash is full, it means things not meant for sight are being disposed of in the proper place. But a full trash can gives off an overwhelmed energy. *Why is there so much trash? Are these people trashy? Are they wasteful?* The answer to the last question is a resounding *yes*. Show me a person who isn't wasteful, and I'll show you a liar. In other countries, possibly. In ours, not likely. The idea of waste doesn't connect with many people. Why would it? The idea of having to use every portion of what you are given is taught as a history lesson in school about some type of man who had more hair than we do today. A trip through the garbage might build a little character for some. My few dumpster dives in life weren't as miserable as they could have been. I was dumb for wearing my father's watch during my second trash escapade. The liquid it was covered in at the bottom of the pile was no liquid I recognized. It took weeks to remove that smell.

Luckily, there's enough light and fresh air in this lobby to keep any unrecognizable liquids from forming. This is where the hugs are given. "Great to see ya" and "How was the week?" tossed into the air to be responded to by anyone within breathing distance. Where the bad news is shared and the "I've been praying for you" comments are exchanged. How many times is that comment true? I never say it because those expectations are too high for me. I prayed for that guy who got in the wreck they mentioned online. I'd hate to go out like that. Let me go out in the peace of my home. Watching my favorite TV show. Not on the TV like that. People do seem to be praying hard for that little girl too. She's kind of energized the troops. Another reason I didn't have any of my own: losing one would be too much for me to carry. It feels like she's set up for one of those unexplainable miracles, though; their family seems holy enough for that level of blessing.

The lobby is one of the few places I get noticed. People come up and "thank you for all you do" me to death. I act like it doesn't matter, but a little appreciation goes a long way. Almost every interaction is positive. Except for the ones with Jonah. I wonder if he thinks he's funny when he comes and tells me I missed a few spots in the offices. I don't know why he's allowed back there anyway; I understand he's the pastor's kid, but he's clearly a brat. I like to keep all lobby conversations short, no matter if they are praise or "correction." When I do show up, I need to get to my spot in the auditorium. I don't need any new folks taking my row. I need the AC to brush me just right. No need for me to sit in hell while I'm trying to make it to the other place.

Day: Saturday, November 6
Time: 5:35 a.m.
Location: Grace Jenkins Memorial Hospital

Do I look as old as the rest of the people in this lobby?

Sheesh. I need to die then.

I've lived a full life. There haven't been many things I didn't try once. I was a curious soul—you always knew that. I always came back around to you, though. I've known life is better with you for decades now.

There were probably some people I could have treated better, definitely some guys I could have at least called back. They were always trying to hold my hand and own me, though. I'm not to be owned. I'm to be adored.

I loved and lost several people, but I'm really hoping I get to see some of them again after we talk, Lord.

Source: Harriett Wallard, 92

Day: Sunday, November 7
Time: 5:59 p.m.
Location: Ramezus Living Room

That was the perfect Halloween costume. I haven't been an intern for so long but it was fun to play one again. Better yet, all it took was an intern name tag, pants that don't fit, and an unironed shirt. My father would have never let me show up to work with a shirt with wrinkles. That would have been a quick smack on the back of my head. Parents get in trouble for hitting their kids these days, but the fear of that smack helped me make better decisions in life, no question about it. Still, the best decision I ever made was showing up in the lobby of this company thirty-two years ago with no clue how to get in. But that's the sweetness of life, half the battle is just showing up … and leaving the rest up to you has worked for me so far.

Help me enjoy these last two months in my second home as much as possible.

Amen.

Source: Rangar Ramezus, 64

DAY: MONDAY, NOVEMBER 8
TIME: 8:17 P.M.
LOCATION: ZEN HOME OFFICE

My little babies are almost one, God. What a miracle that is.

Two for the price of one ... my head could barely comprehend that news. But you've given me a wife who did it all so flawlessly. She amazes me every day. These kids amaze me every day. Already crawling and stumbling around everywhere. I could watch them fall all day and not get tired of it. I see how strong your love for us is now that I'm a dad. I can't imagine life without them now. Please help me be the best dad I can be. I can't stand the feeling of not knowing what I don't know, and I felt that often this year. Help me trust in my abilities to care for my kids and my wife. Help me never grow tired of sacrificing for them and putting them first in my life.

I praise and love you for each day I get to be a father and husband.

Source: Wayne Zen, 36

DAY: TUESDAY, NOVEMBER 9
TIME: 7:43 A.M.
LOCATION: JACK COS. BBQ RESTAURANT BACK OFFICE

This is not how I wanted it to go this year. All the hope I had at the beginning of the year has turned to anxiety.

She has to feel I'm not comfortable with the pace we're moving at, so does that mean she's become so self-absorbed throughout all of this she can't see me anymore? It's like she's a speeding train, and if I don't get on, I'll be run over. Or worse, kicked off.

This conversation is not going to go well. I can see that. But it has to be had. Help me give it with grace and love.

Source: Graham Curtis, 30

DAY: WEDNESDAY, NOVEMBER 10
TIME: 6:15 P.M.
LOCATION: HAMPTON MALL

Please break through with Zayn. He needs it. He's become the bad tomato of our group. His presence in the room influences everyone else too, which scares me. I can tell he doesn't think we are worth his time, which maybe he's right on that, but we are all on your time and plan. He wouldn't be in the meetings if you didn't want him there. Open his eyes to that. Open his ears to the words we all share in the space. Help him see that you are in the room with us.

Source: Chelsea Elling, 59

DAY: FRIDAY, NOVEMBER 12
TIME: 12:14 A.M.
LOCATION: FAULKNER BEDROOM

I can't stand to look at her anymore. She doesn't look like my sister anymore; she already looks like a ghost of herself.

Is this how everyone looks when they die? My parents don't want to say it and act like a miracle is gonna happen, but I know. I know you already decided to let my sister die. You've just been dragging it out for months. This isn't how they painted you in Sunday school. They don't talk about these parts in the Bible. Is her suffering supposed to help us? Is her pain supposed to bring us together? My parents can barely talk to each other, and they mainly tell me lies at this point.

I want this to be over.

Source: Salem Faulkner, 15

Day: Saturday, November 13
Time: 9:28 a.m.
Location: Crimson Park Trail

God, I think Salem is getting worse. It seems silly to try and correct him on his work when I know his mind is so far from it. It's starting to feel bigger than I can handle. I've been lucky so far with none of my students going through something like this. Divorces, sure. Those are so common these days. But this is worse. This is harder to explain away.

I pray for good news for that family. I pray for anything that uplifts Salem.

Source: Angel Zombuka, 28

Day: Sunday, November 14
Time: 9:45 a.m.
Location: Chaucer Bedroom

That was a big phone call yesterday. I remember when I only dreamed a phone call like that would come in for us. It feels like momentum. It feels like we are starting to round the corner.

I can't thank you enough for that.

Now, can you help make my husband embrace the success we are starting to have with the agency? Or as he always likes to call it, the Oak. "Because oak trees are always sturdy and reliable, just like the agency will be." It's like he doesn't want to smile with me anymore. I'm not supposed to compete with the other people or groups in his life, I love the Bible study too, but he likes to talk about the men in that group more than about us. About everything we are doing.

I miss my hype man.

Source: Veronica Chaucer, 36

DAY: MONDAY, NOVEMBER 15
TIME: 2:42 P.M.
LOCATION: ROSE MOUND MIDDLE SCHOOL BUS DRIVER PARKING LOT

Jesus, bless you for these upcoming breaks.

I can tell I need one; I'm losing my voice too often from yelling at these wild kids.

They always get antsy around the holidays—all that sugar their parents let them eat. If their parents saw how they acted on my bus they would be terrified. I'm afraid to walk back there and see what type of bodily fluids have been put on my seats.

Give me that extra patience juice until the end of the semester. Control these unruly kids and help their parents be better parents. For real.

Source: Alfred Santorin, 58

DAY: TUESDAY, NOVEMBER 16
TIME: 7:19 P.M.
LOCATION: FERMINGTON BACKYARD

Why would my mom suggest "getting another hobby"?

Music is my life. The band is my life. It's how I live for you and how I connect with the people around me.

I know this year hasn't been what we planned or wanted, but that's the story of all bands. They all go through something. They all fall apart at some point.

Honestly, even if I never make music with the crew again, I just want to go to 7-Eleven and get Slurpees with them.

I can make music by myself, but I can't do life by myself. Help me be a better friend to the people around me.

Source: Trevor Fermington, 17

DAY: WEDNESDAY, NOVEMBER 17
TIME: 11:39 P.M.
LOCATION: BARNES KITCHEN

Jesus, sometimes this world doesn't seem to want us. Sometimes it feels as if your church doesn't want us either. I know they want you to be White with blue eyes to make them feel more comfortable, but that's not the truth. They've always liked their version of the truth, though, and went out of the way to make that *the* truth.

I thought the church was supposed to be for every man and woman of every tongue and nation?

They want to send missionaries to our neighborhoods so they don't have to see how the people they fund keep our neighborhoods persecuted.

I guess the examples of you breaking cultural barriers to reach lives with love and care are the parts of the Bible they skim through.

Source: Harrison Barnes, 32

Day: Thursday, November 18
Time: 7:14 a.m.
Location: Garland Bedroom

More fake thankfulness coming up ... well, I am thankful that our church is growing enough that we don't have to scrum through the offering each week—I'll leave that up to Asher.

He looked so stunned when I walked into the office and saw him going through the safe. What a drug addict. Yeah, sure he was adding his own money to the pot.

That's how I know the entire idea of church is a facade—our worship pastor is addicted to painkillers and people look up to him in our church. That's why I don't look up to any of our elders because I know they are as broken as everyone else. I'll look up to you and I pray that you are always the standard in my life, not anyone here on Earth.

His secret is safe with me as long as he doesn't tell anyone I go back there to sleep during service. My dad isn't telling me anything he doesn't already stuff down my throat at home.

Source: Jonah Garland, 16

Day: Friday, November 19
Time: 4:01 p.m.
Location: Metzen Bedroom

I'm sorry, God.

I see the stress I've been putting on my mom this year with my actions. I've been selfish, I admit that. I always pictured a life that included only me and my mom, but I never let her edit that photo. Or put anyone else in it. She's done everything for me in my short life, so the least I can do is support her and remember she had a life before I was around.

Kenny is okay. I can learn to get past his disturbing sweater choices and respect him ... enough.

Whatever makes my mom happy—that's what I want.

Source: Hauz Metzen, 15

DAY: SATURDAY, NOVEMBER 20
TIME: 9:09 A.M.
LOCATION: CROOKED HEIGHTS FOOTBALL OFFICES

Just like that, the season is gone.

Three months gone in a blink. Like the end of every season, Father, I pray that I gave these young men someone to look up to. I hope they saw me carry myself like a professional, saw me bring heart to my work every day, saw me care for others and put other people first.

I hope they were able to cherish each moment with their friends and family. There's nothing like football in the fall. There's nothing like walking out of a locker room as a winner. There's nothing like sacrificing for something bigger than yourself.

Some of these kids will never get to play another down of football. I pray that you put something in their lives that keeps them on the right path.

And for all the kids that want to come back and make a name for themselves next year, I hope they're ready for me all summer, baby. Offseason starts today!

Source: Oliver Pernell, 48

DAY: SUNDAY, NOVEMBER 21
TIME: 10:33 P.M.
LOCATION: SALTWATER HALL A MACKENZIE COLLEGE ROOM 101

Help all the people in my dorm travel home safely, God.

This semester is flying by and I can't thank you enough for all the growth you've pulled me through. A year ago I couldn't have imagined myself praying in front of people—better yet, praying at all. Somehow, this seems like what I was always supposed to do. It's a strange feeling, being content with who I am and who I am in you.

I used to want a community where I could be myself. Now I'm creating that and it wouldn't be possible without you.

Thank you for each day where I can live for you.

Source: Kamden Upstin, 19

DAY: MONDAY, NOVEMBER 22
TIME: 9:42 A.M.
LOCATION: AIRPORT SHUTTLE

Finally. Finally, finally, finally. When my parents ask me about my career as soon as I get off the plane, I can tell them that ish is going great.

The girl secured the bag!

Bless you for believing in me when I didn't believe in myself.

Source: Yasmine Armun, 24

Day: Tuesday, November 23
Time: 6:16 a.m.
Location: Tree Stand

I've always been thankful for every week you give us on this great Earth. I'm thankful for crisp, silent mornings like this, for a wife that gives me time to enjoy hobbies, for children that don't think I'm a bad dad for killing Bambi, for a world that doesn't seem completely out of balance when I'm up here.

Help me always cherish these times. I know I won't have them forever, so I'm grateful for each one I do have.

Oh, lookie there, let these hands stay still for a few more moments ....

Source: Chapman Herman, 63

Day: Wednesday, November 24
Time: 3:15 p.m.
Location: Saudiner Kitchen

Give me the courage to be who you made me to be, Lord.

Tomorrow is already gonna be a shit show, so might as well tell my fam what's up.

I don't want to lie anymore. I don't want my entire life to be centered around a mask hiding who I really am. I understand that it will change everything about my relationships with them, but it will be worth it. This inner me will drown me if I don't tell them. If I don't tell myself, really.

Cheers to a drunk Thanksgiving.

Source: Dustin Saudiner, 21

DAY: THURSDAY, NOVEMBER 25
TIME: 11:24 A.M.
LOCATION: BRANSON AND FIFTY-SEVENTH STREET

What am I supposed to be thankful for? These Tooney housing projects I hear rumors about in the streets sound like something to be thankful for, but they won't be here tomorrow. I don't know if I'll survive until the doors open on them. At least someone's thinking of us, though.

Thankfulness isn't as simple as people try to sell it. Everyone is only thankful because you take care of them in their silk sheets and plush pillows. Those are the same people who go to the food drive and serve us turkey scraps before they go home to their four-course meals.

If they shared their turkey legs with a dog like I do now they wouldn't post pictures of themselves at the dinner table. All that's left is this dog who thinks I'm supposed to take care of her now too. She has made me laugh a few times this month. That's something I haven't done in a while. If anything, I believe she's thankful for me. The little love, the little care that I can give her, she appreciates. She doesn't see me as a homeless person. She sees me as her person. She claims me. And that's enough some days.

Source: Ulises Zind, 42

Day: Friday, November 26
Time: 8:18 p.m.
Location: Morton Bath

My favorite type of Friday: the kind where work is never on your calendar.

Bless holiday weekends, bless holiday shopping deals, bless leftovers, and bless you, Jesus. And I knew you would come through for the Garlands. You gotta look out for the good people down here; the bad people get enough of the breaks.

Source: Quincy Morton, 33

Day: Saturday, November 27
Time: 9:44 p.m.
Location: Target Aisle 13

This time next year I want to be thankful for relationships in the industry, for studio time that doesn't make me go into debt, for songs that celebrate life, for a family who believes in my dreams because they are becoming tangible, for streams that make me feel worthy of that dream, for a reason to keep going besides the half truth that I have nothing else to give.

Let my mustard seed move these mountains in front of me, God.

Source: Booker Naheem, 22

DAY: SUNDAY, NOVEMBER 28
TIME: 10:50 A.M.
LOCATION: NEW HAVEN AUDITORIUM

Thanks for letting us gather in your name today, Father. It's not lost on me how lucky we are to live in this time and place where we can worship you without fear of persecution.

It has been an honor to lead the Many Men Bible Study this year and it has grown and pushed me toward a closer relationship with you, and that's invaluable to me. I feel like you're calling me to let it go and let someone else lead it, though, and selfishly, that's not what I want. I want to be in the trenches with the guys, but you opened my eyes this week with where I should really be putting in the time: with my wife. I felt terrible having to learn of the amazing news about the business through the newsletter. I've been absent all year for her, and that's not what I promised her or myself. I need to get back to being her support beam in everything she builds. Let me be better for her moving forward.

I pray the study lives on without me and the guys continue to stay true to your word and your kingdom.

Source: Keith Chaucer, 35

DAY: MONDAY, NOVEMBER 29
TIME: 3:42 P.M.
LOCATION: NEW HAVEN OFFICES

Well, that was not my best Sunday.

At least I get another one this week, right?

Some days I'm convinced this is not the life for me. How can I preach these things about how great a father you are to us, but I can't convince my own son to open up to me?

When did his attitude become so unhelpful and actively rude? I know I'm far from perfect, but I'm trying my best. He'll see when he becomes a dad how all the answers you thought were verified become open to interpretation. How nothing is quite as certain as you think ... except for you.

Help my household and my church overcome my shortcomings and be committed to the Great Commission ... with or without me at the helm.

Source: Marcus Garland, 44

DAY: TUESDAY, NOVEMBER 30
TIME: 1:29 P.M.
LOCATION: MINTERSON COUNTY POLICE STATION

Six years. Six years since the best decision of my life. This job has given me so much and pushed me in ways I didn't know were possible.

It has forced me to rely on you in ways I wasn't capable of, and for that I'll forever be in debt to this place. I don't know how much longer I'll be here, or any police job for that matter, but while I'm still standing and people still need help, I pray you help me use this badge to the best of my abilities.

Source: Danielle Grainger, 33

DAY: WEDNESDAY, DECEMBER 1
TIME: 5:36 P.M.
LOCATION: BRANCH BACKYARD

Why did my mom not stop the car? I get it. But I still don't like it.

That was Juniper with that homeless person. I know it was. She looked so bad! All dirty and cold like that. They said it was my job to take care of her and now they aren't letting me do that. We can go save her right now. But they want me to believe that she's "right where she's supposed to be." I feel like I did all the hard work and someone else gets the credit of her dog kisses and hugs.

I guess that homeless person probably could use some dog love. It sucks that it has to be Juniper's, though. I hope she's the best dog for him. And I hope he sees how lucky he is to have her. How lucky we both were.

Source: Miles Branch, 10

Day: Thursday, December 2
Time: 11:30 a.m.
Location: Tooney Farms

I hate this time of year. It reminds me of everything I can't afford, especially in this house. Sorry, *estate*. Everything I know my son wants but doesn't ask for because he already understands where we are in life. I never wanted him to feel that—that poorness in his heart. He deserves so much better.

For once in my life, I want Santa to hit our house in full. No small Christmas, no empty stockings. You know I'll do whatever it takes to keep us afloat. I don't love my actions, but the results are better than what you are providing us. I'm only dealing with the cards you've given me. You can't be mad at me for that.

I'm sorry I don't see any other way to provide for us right now. Don't give up on us.

Source: Toni Gentle, 39

DAY: FRIDAY, DECEMBER 3
TIME: 8:08 A.M.
LOCATION: ABBERNATHY BEDROOM

No one can tell me you aren't good. In everything I see your touch. I see you moving in these kids I speak to. I see you moving in the fellas back in the hole. I see you moving in my surroundings and circumstances. But I know you and your plan for me are bigger than any circumstance I may find myself in. Right now, though, the circumstance I'm in feels like it's right where you want me to be, and I haven't felt that in years.

You've brought me through the valley, Lord, so please give me the endurance to climb the mountain.

I love you and I hope I can serve you with every breath.

Amen.

Source: Oscar Abbernathy, 61

DAY: SATURDAY, DECEMBER 4
TIME: 1:31 P.M.
LOCATION: 4522 BRIGGUM STREET

I don't know anymore ... Rudy's switching up his damn shop. It's almost not worth the effort to keep this high, but the pain isn't worth it either.

I'm too much of a coward to ask for help. I never had that David confidence. I would have watched him go into battle and wished him well from the tent.

I only see this ending one way.

Please let her forgive me.

Source: Asher Sage, 38

Day: Sunday, December 5
Time: 6:32 p.m.
Location: Haranna Dining Room

Father, thank you for this Sunday dinner my amazing daughter cooked tonight. Thank you for these moments we are able to spend together as a family—as an entire family, because we know she is right here with us, wondering why her son and I didn't help Estella with the food. But we all know it's better when we stay out of the kitchen. We wish she was with us, but I can't think of a better guardian angel to have watching over us.

I'm grateful for these kids who have taken better care of me the past two years than I have of them. Help me be better for them.

I pray for a great week for all of us.

In your name we pray, amen.

Source: Ivan Haranna, 74, Leo Haranna, 37, and Estella Haranna, 40

Day: Tuesday, December 7
Time: 1:27 p.m.
Location: Camden First Bank

Whew. I'm not sure where those fishes came from, but we needed the entire net this time. You just like to see me stress and worry for a few months each year, don't you? That's our fun little pattern. I'd love to not replay this one next year, though. We are due for a breakthrough. Marcus is going to love putting this one in a future message.

If I can put one more at the top of the list for you, help Jonah see that we love him no matter how he feels. Inside and outside of the church.

Source: Emory Garland, 48

Day: Wednesday, December 8
Time: 8:48 p.m.
Location: Luper Campus Library Mackenzie College

Help me pass these finals I'm not ready for. Help me perform better on the court. Help me be me.

This semester has not been my finest ... at all. It's like all the momentum I had going in life turned on me and is trying to blow me out now. Every decision I make is questionable, every move I make is the hardest one, every joke I make isn't funny ... I promise I was funny in high school. These girls have a terrible sense of humor, that's the only explanation for that.

I can't remember the last week I had where I got to Sunday and didn't feel burned out. It probably doesn't help that I barely have time to go to church and spend time with you on Sundays anymore as well. I'm sorry for pushing you to the back burner, but there's so much on my plate right now.

I need this break. I need to spend time at home. And I need to eat some of my dad's food.

God, help me be the best student-athlete I can be. Help me be the best version of Layla.

Source: Layla Sacron, 18

CHAPTER TEN
The People

The hardest thing for me to clean. They're always changing and growing and shrinking and mocking me for my inability to scrub the dirt off their soul. The outside can be cleaned, sure, but the inside is the part that escapes me. That's why I'm better with a mop and soap than messages and scripture. No matter how hard I want everyone to shine like I know they can, some people can't shake the mud they're stuck in. There is no secret formula. No heavy-duty cleanser. No magical eraser that can wipe clean the stains on the inside. I guess that's why they go to church. To get clean on the inside.

The worst part about an internal cleanse is that no one can notice it. That's the joy of my job. Making things new again. Seeing the proof in the pudding brings me back to the buffet each week with a smile on my face. But the type of cleaning that goes on within the people of New Haven, or any church, isn't noticeable on first review. The only person who knows if they are truly clean or not is the person who threw themselves into the water. They can't walk around with a Clean sign on their forehead because that would make most believe the opposite. They're supposed to live it out. How do you live out clean when everything around you is dirty? The people. The air. The water. The relationships. You take two steps as a clean individual and get splashed by the car zooming by full of insecurities and broken promises. What might be worse about an internal clean is that you can fake it. It's not easy scrubbing your soul clean, so some people act like it was never dirty in the first place. You can try to cover it up on the outside with charity and kindness, but I see through it. I know the rot is taking over on the inside. I can feel the mold taking hold.

I wish I could do something about it. But I can't. I have to leave that cleanse to the Big Man upstairs. I wonder if he gets tired of all the cleaning. Or of all the repeat washes. Rinse and repeat. Rinse and repeat. All that washing gives him the chance to get to know us. Well, more like gives us the chance to get to know him. To see his care for us. To feel it every time he removes the stains. To laugh at how he knows our dirtiest spots without needing to ask. To appreciate his grace every time we come back needing the same dirt removed. To spend time in his presence. To get to know him on a first-name basis.

DAY: THURSDAY, DECEMBER 9
TIME: 6:11 A.M.
LOCATION: BYRDWOOD BEDROOM

This one is going to hurt our church, Lord, I know it.

Tragedies like these are the type that break people—from the inside out. And they break the faith in people.

It's different for me. I've been around death, and life, enough to know that even with all of the medical advances we have at our fingertips, some things are out of our hands. But the people who don't work in this field spend the majority of their lives thinking they have control of their futures, their work, their fate, until that one diagnosis changes their life and rips it all away from them. Suddenly, all the power they had is stripped from them and it creates a vacuum in their life. Some people are lucky and allow you to fill that space. Others aren't, and they spiral to dark places with nothing to fill that hole.

I want you to work a miracle and save Izzy's life so that doesn't happen to anyone, I do ... but what I want more is for people to remain faithful to you no matter the outcome of her life, or anyone's.

Source: Percy Byrdwood, 50

Day: Friday, December 10
Time: 9:39 p.m.
Location: Chaucer Living Room

Thank you for weeks like this one. For a birthday with my hubby's undivided attention. Whatever you did there, it worked. I wasn't going to ask for an apology, but it's still nice to get one. And what a lovely little surprise Christmas party to get us started for our future "office holiday parties." That's the wind I was missing behind me too. Help me never take him for granted.

Amen.

Source: Veronica Chaucer, 37

Day: Saturday, December 11
Time: 10:33 p.m.
Location: Norman Living Room

Hmmm, what do you think?

I don't hate it, but I don't love it. Rudy's Crafts & Cocktails. It does have a nice ring to it.

Beginning again has already been as stressful as imagined, but the memories I'm creating with my family will make it all worthwhile.

Bless this new adventure we're taking and give us the wisdom to make the right decisions and the courage to make them happen. Thank you for all the trials coming our way, I know they will only make us stronger in the end.

Help me be patient as we put all these puzzle pieces together. And I pray the final picture is more beautiful than we can imagine.

Amen.

Source: Rudy Norman, 38

DAY: SUNDAY, DECEMBER 12
TIME: 9:09 A.M.
LOCATION: JOYCE BEDROOM

It's starting to feel like you only bless those who are close to you. I've made strides this year on my relationship with you, but I feel like I don't see any of the benefits that are supposed to come with my obedience. Everything is still hard. My mom is still on me to be better, my teachers are still on me to be better, my friends are still on me to care less—everyone wants something from me. I forget what I want sometimes. Really, I never knew what I wanted in the first place. I want you to protect me, but I don't want you to keep me from the things in this world we aren't supposed to "covet."

Why can't I have money? Why can't I have influence? At least I can be honest that those things are attractive to me.

Help me want what you want, God.

Source: Zehare Joyce, 16

DAY: MONDAY, DECEMBER 13
TIME: 5:18 P.M.
LOCATION: BERTON DOG PARK

God,

This has been a difficult lesson. Even for me. And I'm all about lessons. I don't know what's going to happen with Izzy, that's up to you, but I know Salem will need people to love on him no matter what.

I've always been Miss Professional with my students, but you've taught me how to be personal with my kids through this saga. They need more than some red marks sometimes. Let me be an open ear and shoulder to lean on for Salem. And a badass tutor.

Amen.

Source: Angel Zombuka, 29

DAY: TUESDAY, DECEMBER 14
TIME: 11:58 A.M.
LOCATION: HOMELAND MANUFACTURING PACKING ROOM

A lot of lasts these days—the last Monday. Last Tuesday. Last full week.

I don't wanna shed any tears at the office Christmas party this Friday, Father. I haven't cried once in all these years, except during the cuts. Those were angry tears more than anything. That was the closest I ever was to leaving this place. Those people—my friends— they deserved better. I was thankful to keep my job, of course, but I hate it had to happen that way. I'm glad we never had to do that again. One week of that was enough for a lifetime. I got lucky a lot at this job over the years, now that I think about it. You were always looking out for me when I didn't know what to look for.

One thing I need you to answer for me now: What the heck am I gonna do with all this time?

Source: Rangar Ramezus, 64

DAY: WEDNESDAY, DECEMBER 15
TIME: 4:04 P.M.
LOCATION: GRACE JENKINS MEMORIAL CAFETERIA

This is serious, Lord, the people in this hospital deserve better pudding than this. This is some of the worst pudding I've had in a long time, and I'm super old. At least brighten this place up with a little taste. That little girl skipping around the hallway the other day was a bright spot, for sure. You could tell she hadn't been disappointed in life at all. Such a beautiful smile. She doesn't deserve to be here. And from the looks of her parents behind her, they had spent too much time around here as well. Their son looked like the only one who knew where he was—a place for the soon-to-be-dead folks.

I don't know what she has or how serious it is, but I pray it never takes away her light.

And for me, I hope you take my light swiftly. I can tell I'm barely a flicker these days. Who would have thought my flame would ever dim? For a while I thought you had cursed me to live forever, but turns out you have a good sense of humor.

Thank you for all the pudding you've put in my life. Thank you for all the life you've put in my life.

See you on the other side.

Source: Harriett Wallard, 92

DAY: THURSDAY, DECEMBER 16
TIME: 12:12 P.M.
LOCATION: ROSE MOUND MIDDLE SCHOOL CAFETERIA

Jesus, thanks for Thursdays with my friend.
For snowy Decembers.
And tables with no gum on them.
And chairs with even legs.
For short lunch lines.
For extra chocolate milk in the back.
And extra-long Christmas breaks.
And nice presents from Santa.
But mainly for your birthday.
Yeah, the real reason for the season.
Finally, bless this bread.
Oh, that's good.
I know, right? I heard my parents say it the other day. Amen.
Amen.

Source: Bryce Loon, 14, and Louis Dander, 14

DAY: FRIDAY, DECEMBER 17
TIME: 6:44 A.M.
LOCATION: TOONEY FARMS

Your gifts to us have always been the sweetest. The birth of
your son was always going to be the gift that we couldn't repay.
You sacrificed so much for us to be able to come back into your
kingdom and I still don't think we can understand how powerful
that gesture was, and is, as mere humans. We have the great ability
of minimizing all the miraculous things you do in our lives, big and
small, as humans.

I know your son was the ultimate gift, but I hope our gift back
to this community can have an ounce of the impact that did. It's

a more than generous gift by most measures, people will probably say we lost our good judgment, but I'm more worried about eternal judgment than any opinions here on Earth.

I pray that our gift to the city outlasts us for many years to come and that it always stands for something bigger than our family. It's about this community. This place. These people.

Praise you for the ability to make such a gift.

Amen.

Source: Fallon Tooney, 71

DAY: SATURDAY, DECEMBER 18
TIME: 9:41 A.M.
LOCATION: FURTAN MAILBOX

This system is backward. How is it that the people who can't afford the bills end up getting stuck with them? Every doctor in that place could take care of these bills for us in five minutes. But these are gonna hang over my family for years. They take advantage of people when they are sick and in pain, right when they need someone to lift them up, not dig them farther into a ditch. There isn't enough money from any of our jobs to outrun these payments. We are barely getting by as is.

We need a Christmas miracle, God. Show us your warmth and power. Keep this from being the beginning of a long, cold winter.

Source: Benny Furtan, 22

DAY: SUNDAY, DECEMBER 19
TIME: 8:04 P.M.
LOCATION: CURTIS SHOWER

I can't believe a whole year has already gone by. We were in a much different place when this year started, and now we are … here. I don't know where *here* is, though. The only way to describe *here* is baby-less. We got some big answers this year, which I am thankful for, but they led to bigger questions. Mainly: How far is my husband willing to go to make me happy? He's always gone above and beyond for me, but things are different now. We are on different paths for the first time in a long time, and it scares me. I know he tried to talk about it last month, but we don't have time to talk about it for two years like we did two years ago. I *can't* do this without him, literally, but I don't *want* to do it without him either. He makes me feel whole, but a baby would make *us* feel whole.

Whatever we are going through right now, just push us through this. Push us past this and to the point where we are bringing home our baby for the first time.

Source: Tricia Curtis, 32

DAY: MONDAY, DECEMBER 20
TIME: 10:16 P.M.
LOCATION: JACK COS. BBQ RESTAURANT BACK OFFICE

It's okay. I'm fine with it. I've always wanted whatever makes her happy and if I can't be the one to make that happen then I can accept that path if that's our future, but I'm not going down that road without a fight. This will be the hardest fight of my life, but she's worth it. She's worth whatever struggle is in front of us. *Our* future baby is worth it.

Source: Graham Curtis, 30

DAY: TUESDAY, DECEMBER 21
TIME: 11:17 P.M.
LOCATION: GRANT BEDROOM

Don't let these PC officers keep us from *our* Christmas.

It's not "the holidays," it's Christmas. They are getting off work because of you. They are getting drunk because of you. At least be honest about the whole thing and admit they owe you one.

I'll never forget the reason for the season, and I'll never forget what my dad told me about this month all those years ago: this is when everyone is proud to be an American and enjoy our festivities and parties, but wait till things go sideways and the pretenders fall out from the contenders for supporting Christ and America.

Father—never let me be a pretender for you. Keep me honest all my days.

I love you, and I look forward to Santee Claus.

Source: Austin Grant, 58

DAY: WEDNESDAY, DECEMBER 22
TIME: 8:44 P.M.
LOCATION: GRACE JENKINS CHILDREN'S HOSPITAL

Pleeeeeease make sure Santa can make it to my room at the hospital, Jesus. I told Mommy and Daddy that he only goes to houses but they said he might show up here ... in person! I don't believe it because he's too busy getting all the other kids their gifts—he wouldn't have time to stop just for me.

I'll still leave some cookies out just in case. I don't want to make him feel like I forgot him.

I hope he remembers what I wrote him. And Salem and Mommy and Daddy's gifts too.

Source: Izzy Faulkner, 7

DAY: THURSDAY, DECEMBER 23
TIME: 6:11 P.M.
LOCATION: NEW HAVEN BREAKOUT ROOM

I can't believe Chelsea got me a gift. After the way I've treated her and the entire group this year, why would she do that? Now I look terrible for not getting her anything. Or anyone here. But that's my brand: take and never give. I've taken all these people's pity prayers this year. I've taken their doughnuts. Their time. And now their Christmas gifts. What am I supposed to give them? I have nothing to give. I don't have money. I don't have a "network" to tap into for things.

Maybe Chelsea is right, maybe I don't owe this group anything, but I owe everything to myself … I owe it to myself to give me another chance. That's all I have to give anyway. But that has always been the hardest thing for me to do, give myself a second chance.

I guess it's time to give in to The Second-Chance Class.

Source: Zayn Niro, 44

DAY: SATURDAY, DECEMBER 25
TIME: 5:00 P.M.
LOCATION: LANSING LIVING ROOM

We praise you for another day to celebrate your birth, Lord. We should be celebrating your life-changing story every day because it changes our lives every day. We wouldn't be able to do what we can without your love and hands constantly molding us to be the perfect piece of clay for our current place in life. I've lived a full life and I forget you still have plans for these old bones some days, but I know if I'm still breathing you need me here.

I'm always here for Maleek, but I don't know if he knows that—or if he wants to know that. I hope he has a warm meal and feels love around him wherever he is on this Christmas Day.

Look after everyone who doesn't have anyone today, Lord. Amen.

Source: Gigi Lansing, 83

DAY: SUNDAY, DECEMBER 26
TIME: 11:45 P.M.
LOCATION: METZEN KITCHEN

Our first Christmas together as a *family* ... and we didn't break anything. I call that a success.

This year hasn't been great all the time—I haven't been great all the time—but I think we can be great together.

I love this woman. And I love her son.

Don't ever take them from me. Teach me how to put them first in my life.

Source: Kenny Sturgiss, 38

DAY: MONDAY, DECEMBER 27
TIME: 12:55 A.M.
LOCATION: ROUGHSHED BASEMENT

The first Christmas without him didn't feel right. There was too much silence, too much calm. I forgot how loud he was. Ha. We needed that in our family.

He was always the one who knew how to speak up; he left a vacuum there. I could barely speak up before, and now I don't have the energy or the desire, or whatever that feeling in your heart is that tells you it's time to step up. I haven't felt that since he left us. That drive in me was taken when he went on his last drive.

I want to ask you to help me move on, but that's not what I want. I don't want to move on from him. I want to move on with him. Am I supposed to feel like this? No one else seems to be struggling so much—or they aren't showing it. I wear it on my sleeve. The best I can do is learn to live with it, so that's what I'll ask: help me learn to live with him next to you instead of next to me. I know that's a better place than anywhere down here. Help me achieve everything we were supposed to do together. Let me carry on our name with a new purpose.

Source: Nick Roughshed, 26

Day: Tuesday, December 28
Time: 9:15 a.m.
Location: Garland Bedroom

Thank you for waking me up today.

Please use my life to live a real Christian life. Not what you see in movies or TV, not what you see onstage or in the pamphlets, but what it really looks like to build your kingdom. I can take the jokes and side comments and being uninvited from the kickback, but I can't take the false imagery around our faith. Things in life aren't magically perfect for us when we accept you into our hearts. Our bank accounts don't magically fill up, our parents don't magically understand how to communicate with us, we are just as messed up as everyone else. We just accept that we have you to bring all of our problems to first. Not that you will fix every problem, but you help us see we aren't defined by them. We aren't our sin, we aren't our selfishness, we aren't our pride, we aren't our lies—you cover all those things with your blood. I don't know how to say that though. My dad's the speaker and I can tell he already wants me to follow in his footsteps, but you know that's not me. I have to find my own way. I have to find my own truth in this because his truth doesn't represent me.

I know I can be a better son to my parents, but I want to be a better Christian first. Please help me be that person.

Source: Jonah Garland, 16

DAY: WEDNESDAY, DECEMBER 29
TIME: 11:32 A.M.
LOCATION: NEW HAVEN OFFICES

I hate canceling church, but I know no one understands how to drive with a little bit of dust on the ground in this city, so it's better this way.

We'll come back and it will be another turn of the calendar. This time of the year always makes me anxious. I feel like I need a report of how we changed the lives of the kids to show Marcus, so he keeps saying yes when I ask for more funds and events and content and all of it. Just a little ROI dashboard. That's the hard and best part of this role: I never know when I'm doing it right. There's always hope the kids are sincere and are truly turning their hearts toward you, but then there's always the possibility they had a crush on someone else who walked up for extra prayer. They change so much in a year too. Some of them go from innocent and bright youngins to silent and brash teens who think it's cool to never speak at all. It's funny, in a sad way, to see them change and grow up so fast. All I can do is trust in you to be the one making waves in their hearts. I'm only here to be an example of what a life dedicated to you looks like. I pray I never take my position for granted and that I always stay close to you as I try to lift up these kids to you.

Source: Wayne Zen, 36

DAY: THURSDAY, DECEMBER 30
TIME: 6:19 P.M.
LOCATION: GARLAND BEDROOM

I hate ending the year on such a sad note. The Faulkner family didn't deserve the year they just went through. Izzy's life didn't deserve to be taken so soon. She was special.

Unfortunately, this is how you remind us that you give and you take and we are called to remain faithful through it all.

Hearts will be broken from this and you will be doubted. I can only pray for your comfort on the Faulkner family and our entire church family right now. Please help people see the bigger picture in all of this. Help me see it.

I know people will ask me about this and expect an answer they can believe in. But the truth is, this part will always be painful. This hurt and pain is a part of our earthly lives, and we can't escape it as much as we wish we could.

January funerals are always the coldest.

Source: Marcus Garland, 44

DAY: FRIDAY, DECEMBER 31
TIME: 3:45 A.M.
LOCATION: 4522 BRIGGUM STREET

Look what we have here. Me *needing* you. God—help me. Save me.

Source: Maleek Wright, 23

EPILOGUE

This wasn't on my list.

I was supposed to hit my growth spurt this year. I was supposed to enjoy my sixteenth birthday. I was supposed to learn how to sneak out of the garage without waking up my parents. It was going to be a great year. But instead, we just "celebrated" at my little sister's funeral. Why do they try to paint it like that? Is it not okay to be sad? I've already pushed all the sad out of me. I don't have any more. My mom might never run out. I don't know how long it's going to take for her to get over Izzy being gone. All she is, is sadness right now. My dad ... I'm worried about him too. He's the opposite. He's trying to be strong, which I appreciate, but it's all on the outside. I can tell he's hurting as much as mom but doesn't want to show it. Izzy would have hated all of this. She was the one who knew how to shake us all up. How to get us out of bed and going. How to make us smile when we didn't want to. I wish I had that touch. I wish I knew how to make my parents smile like she did. I wish I knew how to make them see that it's going to be okay. Because it is. I don't know why. I don't know how. But every day since her last cough in the hospital I've felt ... a touch.

I don't know if it's her. Maybe it's you, God. Maybe it's both. But it's the warmest touch I've ever felt. Every time I start to get cold and think about all the things I'll never get to do with her, I feel it. All the terrible jokes she was going to tell. All the school bullies I was going to scare away for her. All the stupid fights we were going to get into. All the snitching she was going to do on me. She was such a tattletale. All the storms I was going to comfort her through. All the birthdays. All the graduations. All the trips we were going to take around the world together. But right when my mind starts to drift toward that cold place, I feel the push in the opposite direction. The resistance. And it tells me that we'll still get to do all those things together because she'll be with me. I know everyone says that, and I don't really believe in ghosts, but this is different. I know she is here. I know she'll be proud of me when I make the varsity team this year. She'll laugh at me when I spill food on my shirt. She'll get mad at me when I lie to Mom and Dad. She'll think I'm gross when I bring home my first girl. But she'll eventually warm up to her. Because that's what she did for everyone she was around. She warmed up to them and made them warm up to her in the process. Her warmth will walk with me.

I know people at the funeral were wondering why you would let this happen. I could see it in their eyes. In my parents' eyes. And that's how I felt for most of last year. Pastor Garland did a good job of making everything sound nice, he put a good spin on it. You can't put a good spin on everything, though. Some things don't make sense. Some things are above us. But I think that's why you live above us, and all around us. You fill in the spots we don't know how to define. You take care of us when we don't know how to take care of ourselves. That's why Izzy was so happy all the time. She understood she didn't need to understand everything. I'm the opposite. I was the opposite. I wanted all the answers. I had to know how everything worked. I remember getting frustrated whenever I couldn't figure out how to get to the next level on whatever game I was addicted to that week; I would try for hours and hours to win, then would throw the sticks at the wall when I hit my limit on Ls. Izzy walked in and laughed at me for being mad at a "silly video game," then picked up the controller and beat it with ease. I couldn't understand how. It didn't make any sense. How could she possibly know how to beat a game she never played before? She told me she beat it because she didn't care to beat it. I told her that was a stupid answer and to get out of my room. But now, I get it. She beat the game because she didn't put it on herself to beat it. She was never worried about anything because it wasn't hers to worry about. She didn't need to know all the answers because someone else already had them all, and that was enough for her. You filled in all the gaps for her, so she was never stressed about filling them in herself. I bet her prayers were so relaxed. I hope all the people who were at the funeral can learn from Izzy. I hope all the people who were at the funeral and all the people they know, anyone Izzy could have touched—I hope they pray like Izzy. Like they have a father who already has everything figured out for them. They just need to let you play the game for them.

–Salem Faulkner

THE PEOPLE | THE PRAYERS

Marcus Garland | 1.3, 1.10, 5.2, 7.4, 9.5, 10.10, 11.29, 12.30
Augustus Salister | 1.4
Bri Verdana | 1.5, 2.28, 4.21, 5.28, 7.22, 9.20, 10.31
Izzy Faulkner | 1.6, 2.8, 3.14, 5.3, 8.5, 12.22
Keith Chaucer | 1.8, 4.10, 7.24, 10.8, 11.28
Gigi Lansing | 1.9, 1.30, 4.17, 6.19, 8.28, 10.30, 12.25
Ulises Zind | 1.11, 2.14, 4.22, 6.16, 8.7, 9.22, 10.19, 11.25
Jonah Garland | 1.12, 3.3, 4.6, 6.14, 6.27, 9.15, 11.18, 12.28
Layla Sacron | 1.13, 3.6, 3.7, 4.19, 5.26, 7.5, 9.10, 10.27, 12.8
Michael Faulkner | 1.14, 5.24, 9.28
Kenny Sturgiss | 1.15, 2.24, 4.13, 7.1, 9.18, 12.26
Victor Hanoi | 1.16, 3.20, 10.16
Tricia Curtis | 1.17, 2.22, 4.24, 7.10, 9.23, 12.19
Graham Curtis | 1.17, 2.22, 3.30, 6.4, 8.13, 11.9, 12.20
Hauz Metzen | 1.18, 3.1, 4.26, 7.27, 11.19
Bailey Laslo | 1.19, 5.10, 9.4
Wesley Quino | 1.21, 4.29, 7.11, 9.27
Harrison Barnes | 1.22, 3.24, 7.9, 11.17
Dennis Shanty | 1.23
Cooper Knucks | 1.23

Theresa Franklin | 1.24, 7.30, 9.2
Miles Branch | 1.25, 2.16, 2.21, 8.16, 9.24, 12.1
Oliver Pernell | 1.26, 3.15, 5.13, 8.9, 10.15, 11.20
Mick Taylen | 1.27
Bryce Loon | 1.28, 4.15, 5.27, 8.26, 12.16
Louis Dander | 1.28, 4.15, 5.27, 8.26, 12.16
Quincy Morton | 1.29, 3.19, 5.14, 8.6, 11.26
Chelsea Elling | 1.31, 2.26, 4.5, 5.23, 11.10
Everett Saudiner | 2.1, 3.31, 7.6, 11.2
Yaz Azure | 2.2
Royce Smith | 2.2
Wayne Zen | 2.3, 6.3, 6.30, 9.1, 11.8, 12.29
Alfred Santorin | 2.4, 6.25, 8.4, 11.15
Emory Garland | 2.5, 2.7, 3.4, 5.22, 7.18, 10.18, 12.7
Kamden Upstin | 2.6, 3.13, 4.23, 5.29, 7.12, 10.7, 11.21
Zehare Joyce | 2.9, 4.14, 6.11, 6.22, 6.28, 10.3, 12.12
Xavier Balden | 2.10
Verl Muncy | 2.11, 6.26, 9.7, 10.22
Prentice Truth | 2.12, 11.1
Tanner Rick | 2.13
Willow Rick | 2.13
Estella Haranna | 2.17, 4.27, 6.1, 8.20, 10.25, 12.5
Penelope Metzen | 2.19, 10.11
Angel Zombuka | 2.20, 5.4, 7.3, 9.16, 11.13, 12.13
Yasmine Armun | 2.25, 3.12, 4.16, 5.6, 6.10, 7.2, 11.22
Saul Welter | 2.27
Booker Naheem | 3.2, 4.8, 5.17, 6.24, 8.2, 9.13, 11.27
Beiba Palmandi | 3.8, 8.1, 9.21
Austin Grant | 3.9, 4.1, 5.30, 8.25, 9.3, 12.21
Trevor Fermington | 3.11, 6.8, 7.19, 8.27, 10.5, 11.16
Veronica Chaucer | 3.17, 4.7, 5.7, 11.14, 12.10
Dustin Saudiner | 3.18, 4.25, 6.7, 7.21, 8.29, 10.9, 11.24
Umi Harolds | 3.21
Salem Faulkner | 3.22, 7.8, 8.15, 11.12
Helena Joyce | 3.23, 5.21, 6.22, 7.20, 11.5

Rudy Norman | 3.25, 6.9, 7.28, 10.2, 11.4, 12.11
Benny Furtan | 3.26, 5.19, 8.19, 10.4, 12.18
Danielle Grainger | 3.27, 5.5, 6.17, 7.25, 8.31, 10.12, 11.30
Leo Haranna | 3.29, 5.9, 7.7, 9.14, 12.5
Harriett Wallard | 4.2, 5.11, 6.21, 7.29, 9.19, 11.6, 12.15
Jamison Nineh | 4.3
Ian Junith | 4.9
Asher Sage | 4.11, 4.12, 5.20, 7.13, 9.6, 10.14, 12.4
Zayn Niro | 4.18, 6.6, 7.17, 8.22, 9.30, 12.23
Oscar Abbernathy | 4.20, 5.25, 6.29, 8.8, 9.25, 10.29, 12.3
Chapman Herman | 4.28, 8.14, 11.23
Tanner Roughshed | 4.30
Roxy Faulkner | 5.8, 6.20, 10.20
Nick Roughshed | 5.12, 8.30, 12.27
Mario Leflour | 5.16, 6.15, 8.17
Cat Pollier | 5.18
Elliott Banks | 6.2, 7.14, 8.3, 9.11
Kristen Goldstern | 6.5
Fallon Tooney | 6.12, 7.15, 8.23, 9.29, 12.17
Percy Byrdwood | 6.23, 7.26, 9.8, 10.23, 12.9
Rangar Ramezus | 7.16, 8.18, 11.7, 12.14
Toni Gentle | 8.10, 9.17, 10.24, 12.2
Erik Wachowski | 8.24
Gavin Banks | 9.12
Nasir Holiday | 10.28
Ivan Haranna | 12.5
Maleek Wright | 12.31

ACKNOWLEDGMENTS

Many hurrahs for the wonderful team at Warren Publishing: Melissa Long, Amy Ashby, and Mindy Kuhn. Extra props for Mindy on the cover design because we all know everyone judges a book by its cover. Their overall guidance and commitment to this book made my life easier. Their decision to help me bring this book to reality was easily my favorite decision of 2022.

Cheers to Katherine Bartis for her editorial dedication and notes on the manuscript. We love notes! And taking it back to the beginning, please give a round of applause to Karli Jackson. She will go down in history as the first-ever editor to ever edit my edits. A true professional and lovely human being.

Nothing in my life would happen without the support of my family, a.k.a. the gang. Please feel free to yell at them in the street and tell them they did a wonderful job of raising me. Tiff, your simultaneous care and correction has stood the test of time. You can buy stuff for me as long as you want. Mom, thank you for being a fan when there was not anything to be a fan of. I'll work on the whole grandbaby situation … eventually. Dad, thank you for your constant sacrifice and leadership. We are all here because you are here. To my extended family across the map in Nebraska, Iowa, Texas, and Georgia, I hope our paths cross more often.

To my friends who let me send them bad manuscripts and still said good things about my writing, I cherish you. Even if you don't really read them, it still means a lot.

To Zek, appreciate you, my brother.

To anyone who thinks they deserve a shout-out in here, see you in the next one.

To all the sights and scenes that fill my memory bank, thanks for the wealth.

Finally, to keep with the theme of the book, it's also important for me to recognize anyone who has ever prayed for me. I hope it worked.

9 781960 146465